The Dating Challenge

By B. N. Hale

27 Dates: The Series

The Dating Challenge

The Dating Secret

The Dating Game

The Dating Handbook

The Dating Truth

Table of Contents

Part 4: The Magic Date

Part 5: The Island Date

Part 6: The Dare Date

Part 7: The Doctor Date

Part 1: The Valentine's Date

Chapter 1

"No."

The word slipped out of Kate's mouth before she could stop it, obliterating her future in a single syllable. Jason stared at her, his features frozen in disbelief. She was distantly aware of the collective gasp by those present, but couldn't tear her gaze from her boyfriend, still down on one knee.

She struggled to speak but the word seemed to hang in silence, a brutal rejection that could not be withdrawn. Doubt assailed her and her eyes flicked to the ring, the diamond glittering in its black velvet box. Why had she said it? Had she meant it? *Please tell me I didn't say it*.

They'd met in their senior year of high school, just two years ago. They were paired as lab partners and she'd stolen looks at his chiseled jaw line, wondering as to the sudden source of her luck.

"Do you like biology?" she'd asked.

"I prefer chemistry," he said, his lips twitching into a smile.

She flushed and looked away, but a moment later stole another look. At six feet two he was on the tall side for a soccer player. His brown hair was wavy and thick, just begging for fingers to rake their way through, while his brown eyes were arresting in their intensity. They'd begun dating by the end of the week, and she'd fallen hard.

The memory faded and Kate realized that only a fraction of a second had passed. Jason's expression was just starting to change from surprise to hurt, followed quickly by embarrassment. His eyes darted to the circle of friends standing awkwardly around them, settling on Jason's best friend who stood frozen, a partially unrolled poster in his hands that revealed seven letters, *Congrat*—

She swallowed and forced herself to speak. "Jason, I . . ."

How could she explain it to him? How could she explain it to herself? Jason abruptly stood and shut the ring box, the *snap* causing her to flinch. He smiled and made a joke, but both were forced, and no one laughed. Giving up the pretense, he threw Kate a scathing look and strode to the door. She leapt after him, wondering what she could say to withdraw the rejection. Wondering if she would.

Kate looked at the party, yearning to return to the moment before he'd proposed. Paper hearts hung from the ceiling, fluttering in the breeze from the open door. The candy was also shaped like hearts, as were the banners and the ice in the punch bowl.

Jason had been planning the Valentine's Day party for weeks. He'd been evasive and nervous leading up to the day, but she'd assumed it was due to his classes. How could she have known what he was about to do?

As he stepped onto the porch she caught his arm. He whirled, his eyes burning into hers. She winced and snatched her hand back. Anger and pain washed across his features and his jaw clenched. She wanted to comfort him, but doubt lodged in her throat. He'd professed his love and she'd crushed his hope with two letters.

The silence lasted until he grimaced and left. She remained in the door and watched him walk away, his broad shoulders hunched, anger and confusion wafting off his frame. She wanted to call out to him, to repair what she'd said with three letters, but the same part of her that had said *no* bound her tongue, and her apology went unvoiced as he disappeared into the night.

Chapter 2

One Year Later

Kate stared at her textbook, the words blurring into an endless stream of academic language. Deciphering the text occupied much of her homework time, and she made a mental note not to take another class where the professor assigned a book they had personally written. Her phone buzzed and she glanced at the screen.

She didn't read the text, her eyes drawn to the date on top of her phone. February 14th, one year since she'd watched Jason walk away. She'd dreaded the approach of Valentine's Day with the cold certainty of an impending exam, and spent much of the day holed up in her room, trying desperately not to think of him.

And failing.

She thought of their time together, of his smile, of his touch. But more than that she thought of the time after, when he'd wanted an answer she'd been unable to give. Their relationship had ended abruptly and left her reeling. And here she was, one year later, still without an answer.

Her phone went dark, mercifully removing the reminder that a year had passed. Anger briefly flickered in her chest but could not survive against the numb confusion that still held her bound. Releasing a long sigh, she returned her attention to her textbook.

A knock on the bedroom door caused Kate to look up. She glanced at the clock but it wasn't even five, not yet time for dinner. Curious, she stepped to the door and swung it open. To her surprise it was all three of her roommates.

"Did I forget to do my dishes?" Kate asked.

In the center, Ember folded her arms. "It's an intervention."

Kate smiled faintly. "Aside from Netflix, I don't have any addictions."

"You're addicted to solitude," Marta said. "You haven't been on a date in months."

Kate's smile faded and she retreated to her desk. "I've been busy."

Brittney stepped in after her. "You broke up with Jason because you didn't want to get married. Now you've escaped into your studies."

"I need to focus," Kate said, bending over her book.

"Not tonight," Ember said, her voice changing with her smile.

Kate looked up and frowned. "What does that mean?"

"You have a date," Brittney said smugly.

"In thirty minutes," Marta added.

"Who?" Kate demanded.

Brittney shook her head. "You don't know him."

"It's Valentine's Day," Kate protested. "Who would go on a blind date today?"

Ember grinned and departed, a sly smile on her face. "You'd better get ready!"

Marta followed her, and Kate cast Brittney a pleading look. "Why would you do this to me?"

"Because you need it," she said sympathetically, and slipped from the room.

The door shut with a click and Kate stared at the barrier, wondering when her roommates had gained the upper hand. Although only one was blonde they called themselves the blondes, and the redheaded Ember was clearly their leader. The girl was strikingly beautiful but a danger to any boy that crossed her. One boyfriend had made the mistake of breaking up via text, and she'd broken his car window with a hammer, grabbed his phone and smashed it with said hammer. While he was still in the car.

Marta's parents were from Puerto Rico, and she'd inherited their lovely dark complexion, wavy hair, and brown eyes. She had not inherited a love for everything Puerto Rican, a constant point of contention between her, her parents, and her numerous cousins.

Brittney was the only blonde of the bunch and by far the smartest. She was taller than the others and not as trim, but her sense of humor and intelligence were her best assets. She was fond of disparaging vegetables and praising cookies, of which she could only be described as a connoisseur. She was also the best cook in the house.

Kate liked her roommates—most of the time. They'd been with her through the ending of her relationship, a time that Brittney called "The Age of Jason." They'd pulled together for her, and Brittney had even made her quadruple chocolate lava brownies with devil's ice-cream, assuring her that it was the cure to all. But the taste of chocolate was a temporary remedy that did not fill the void in her chest.

Over the last few months the blondes had begun setting her up on dates, most of which she'd managed to avoid. This time they they'd obviously opted to blindside her at the last moment to prevent her from escaping.

Kate had been looking forward to a night curled up in her bed, trying to figure out if it was too late to call Jason. Now she'd have to pretend to smile at the one guy desperate enough to accept a blind date today. On Valentine's Day.

She considered how she could cancel the date, but the blondes where like pretty pit bulls, and any effort to escape their jaws would be futile. Like when Ember had decided she liked a guy on the lacrosse team, and they had spent two weeks learning the rules, even playing in the park with a group of friends. Ember had dated him for less than a week. The girls still played lacrosse.

Kate glanced toward the window, wondering if she could slip out unseen. Her room was small, but at least it was hers. Movie posters lined the walls, mostly from Harry Potter and Marvel. Her bed sat in one corner with her desk on the opposite side of the room. Books were piled above it, old textbooks with a few favorite novels, the pages still bent from where she'd stopped reading.

She groaned and stepped to her closet. Her roommates may have blindsided her, but they had good intentions. She could endure one night to appease them, especially after all they had done in The Age of Jason.

She chose a nice blue shirt and her comfy jeans. When she was dressed she stepped into the bathroom and added a touch of makeup, pausing to stare into the mirror. Her hair was brown like Marta's, but wavier and longer.

Slender and of average height, there was little remarkable about her except her eyes, which were a striking green. Jason had said they were like emeralds that softened when she smiled. She pushed the memory away and tied her hair back. Then she went into the living room to collect her purse and sneakers.

The house was small but close to campus. With little more than a couch and a TV, the living room was not spacious. The kitchen made up for it, and boasted a stainless steel fridge with matching oven and microwave. As Kate sat on the couch and tied her laces, Ember came from the kitchen.

"You can't wear those," Ember said, her features wide with horror.

Kate didn't stop tying her shoes. "If he doesn't like me in sneakers, he won't like me in heels."

Marta stepped into the living room and her eyes flicked to Kate's feet. "You can't wear—"

Kate threw her a scathing look and Marta just shook her head. Brittney appeared with a leftover slice of pizza from the previous night and her eyes fell to Kate's shoes. Before she could speak Kate raised a finger to her.

"You chose the date. I chose my shoes."

The girls sighed in unison, and Kate smiled in triumph. Ember pouted and sank onto the couch. "Don't blame us if he isn't attracted to you."

"Who is this guy anyway?" Kate asked.

"Reed Hansen," Marta said. "He's a TA for one of my classes."

"A master's student?" Kate asked. She'd expected someone younger. "What does he look like?"

Marta and Ember exchanged a look, and Marta said. "He's cute. I think you'll like him. And he dates a lot."

Kate frowned at her evasive tone. An older student that was "cute" and dated "a lot" didn't bode well for her. She pointed an accusing finger at them but the sound of a car door drew her attention.

"He's here!" Ember said brightly.

Kate stepped to the door and slipped into her coat. Then she caught the handle as the bell rang. She swung the door open to reveal her date. She blinked, surprised to find him very attractive. His hair was black but his eyes a dark blue, a contrast that sent heat into her belly. He was trim with a nice build, and came dressed in jeans and a long-sleeved shirt visible beneath his coat. His lips twitched in amusement as he endured the scrutiny.

"Kate Williams?" he asked.

She nodded and stepped outside, shutting the door before the blondes could interject. "Are we going to a movie?"

"I don't know," he said with a shrug. "What do you want to do?"

She sighed, lowering her opinion of him. Perhaps she could fake a headache to save his feelings before it got too late. "How about dinner and then we catch a movie."

He laughed lightly. "I'm sorry to disappoint, but no movie tonight."

She frowned at the mischief in his tone. "You *do* have a plan."

"I always do," he said with a grin.

She stole a glance at his profile, uncertain what to expect from the evening. "I'm happy to pay for myself."

"Don't worry," he said. He walked her to the car and opened the passenger door for her. "There's no check to split."

She came to a halt with one foot in the car. "What sort of date costs nothing?"

"A fun one," he replied.

Intrigued, she couldn't resist a smile. "Time will tell," she said, and stepped into the car.

Chapter 3

He laughed and shut the door for her. Striding around the car, he stepped into the driver's seat and turned the key. The ancient Camry coughed to life and he spun the wheel, pulling onto the road.

"Nice car," she said.

"Is that sarcasm I hear?"

"No."

He grinned. "Tuition sucks all my money, but this little beauty gets the job done."

"What's your major?"

"Psychology. You?"

"Mechanical Engineering."

He raised an eyebrow. "A smart one?"

"I try," she said. "Do you often go on blind dates?"

"Sometimes," he said. "But usually I prefer to meet the girl and ask her out myself."

"On Valentine's Day?" she pressed.

He grinned and threw her a look. "Truthfully, I like to take Valentine's Day off. Usually a girl gets the wrong impression when I plan so much."

"Then why go with me?"

"Your roommates were quite insistent."

She laughed sourly, imagining Ember handcuffing him until he agreed to take her on a date. As they talked he drove off campus and into Boulder, Colorado, headed north. The winter had been surprisingly warm and the roads were clear, the snow already melting long before it was supposed to. He'd said there was no check to split, but she was still surprised when he passed the bowling alley without sparing it a look, and the theatre. She frowned, confused and intrigued.

She swiveled in her seat to examine him anew. "Just how often do you date?"

"Every week," he said. "Sometimes two or three times."

She frowned. "I didn't take you for that kind of guy."

He laughed. "I don't hold hands or kiss unless I want to date exclusively. And no sex."

"Really?"

"Don't sound so skeptical," he said, feigning a wounded expression.

"Just what kind of guy are you?"

"A good one," he said with a grin. "Are you ready for a game?"

"Game?"

"It will take us a few minutes to get to dinner, and a game will help us get to know each other."

"What sort of game?" she asked as they pulled onto the interstate. Getting on the freeway didn't indicate a destination, but as the miles slipped by she wondered what he intended.

"This one is titled Random Facts About Me," he said. "We take turns sharing things people wouldn't normally know."

"You go first," she said.

He smiled as if he'd expected her response and Kate realized the smile came easy and often. His blue eyes flicked her way and the heat returned. She squashed it and turned her attention to his random fact.

"When I was four I almost died because I tried to fly. I broke my arm and fractured my eye socket."

She burst into a laugh. "What did you jump off?"

"The roof," he said. "My mom was livid."

"I bet she was," she said.

He gestured in her direction. "Your turn."

She considered her past for several moments, but Reed seemed content to wait. He took an exit and headed into the mountains outside of Boulder. She should have been concerned at the obscure destination but surprisingly wasn't.

"When I was twelve I went canoeing with some friends," she said. "My older sister and her friends decided to jump off a cliff next to the river. I wanted to look tough so I went with them."

"How high?"

"About forty feet."

He winced. "Sounds painful."

She laughed in chagrin. "I lost my nerve halfway down and bent my legs, and landed on my side. My sister heard the smack from half a mile up the river."

Reed laughed, causing the Camry to tremble, although she guessed that was just the car's transmission struggling with the incline. She grinned at his response and ran her finger up her side.

"My bruise went from butt to bra line."

"That's the best story I've heard in a while," he said.

She watched his eyes as he spoke. Normally when she told that story a guy glanced at her chest, but he kept his eyes on the road. He'd said no physical contact, but she wasn't sure she believed him.

She'd dated quite a bit before Jason, but now as she looked back they were a blur of similar faces. She'd never met anyone like Reed and couldn't tell if he was feeding her a line or meant what he said.

She'd expected the conversation to be tedious on a first date. On Valentine's Day. Instead the game kept the conversation going in surprising and clever directions. He spoke of his sister and growing up in Tallahassee, Florida. She also shared the obligatory details about her family, her three brothers, her divorced mother and father.

The information was mundane, yet told in the context of the game it seemed exciting. Sharing the basic details of their lives in a series of stories and events made Reed's sister seem real and Kate could actually imagine her. His stories of her were tinged with fondness, suggesting a close relationship.

"She's a senior in high school, now," Reed said. "But she wants to come here for college."

"Because of you?" she guessed.

"Of course," he replied with a smile. "But she's going pre-med, so I expect great things from her."

For the next twenty minutes they continued the game as they ascended the road into the mountains. The sun had just begun to set and the creek next to the road reflected the dwindling light. His smile gained a mischievous tilt, all but inviting her to ask where they were going. Finally, she relented with a sigh.

"Where are we going?" she asked.

"Dinner is always better with a view," he said.

He pulled off the road into a parking lot of a small trailhead. A path disappeared into the trees and a pair of other cars sat in the lot, both bearing overhead racks for hiking gear. Lingering patches of snow were visible, but for the most part it had melted away, revealing a forest of evergreen trees. The fading light danced off the spots of snow and filtered through the boughs to light the trail.

"Are they going to find my body?" she asked.

He laughed and pointed into the trees. "We have half an hour to eat before the next activity."

"Next activity?"

"You'll see."

Reed led her down the trail. She fell into step behind him, her gaze drawn to the forest. She'd enjoyed the outdoors as a youth but had rarely seen such beauty at home. The entire state of Arizona was an oven that baked plants until they died a parched death.

Reed glanced back but seemed content to let her enjoy the walk. Ten minutes later he stepped off the trail and threaded his way through the trees. Her curiosity mounted as she followed, and abruptly stepped onto a ledge that overlooked the valley.

Her eyes widened at the stunning view, and she shielded her gaze from the sun setting in the distance. Endless tracts of land stretched away from them, reaching all the way to the lights of Boulder. Pockets of snow dotted the trees like frosting, and caught the setting sun to make the vista sparkle.

A creek gurgled nearby, cascading over an icy ledge to create a waterfall that plunged down the escarpment. A cool breeze blew across Kate and Reed, rustling the evergreen branches to elicit a shiver.

"How many girls have you brought up here?" she breathed.

"You're the first," he said. "I don't mind repeating date activities, but this one I was saving."

"You should have saved it for a girlfriend," she said, and turned to him.

"I was," he admitted, "but the seasons refused to cooperate. I only have one year left and I wasn't sure I could use it. Couldn't let it go to waste, now could I?"

She joined him on a fallen log and tightened her coat about her. Spring had begun its triumph, at least on the south side of the slope. The dazzling sunset lent a warmth to the air that robbed winter of its lingering sting.

"The weather is perfect," she said with a smile.

She turned away from the sunset to find him picking up a cooler he'd stashed behind the log. Complete with sandwiches, chips, and a drink, it was an entire picnic without the basket. He then withdrew a blanket and covered the log, gesturing an invitation. She took a seat next to him as he withdrew two sandwiches.

"What is all this?" she asked.

He grinned, his eyes sparkling with humor. "Welcome to dinner."

Chapter 4

"I can't believe you did this," she said.

"Why?" he asked. "Turkey or roast beef?"

"Turkey," she finally said. "And what if I was a vegetarian?"

"You aren't," he said, handing her the turkey sandwich. "I asked Marta."

"Are all your dates so detailed?" she asked, skewering him with a look.

He smiled and took a bite, his answer coming out muffled. "Always."

"Why?" she repeated, gesturing to the food and the view. "You don't even know me."

He laughed easily. "Perhaps I enjoy seeing a girl smile."

"And that's *all* you want?" she asked.

His laughter echoed off the cliff. "Not all guys are dogs."

"That's not enough of an answer," she said. "I want to know why you would do all this." She took a bite of her sandwich and waited.

He raised a hand as if to forestall her suspicion. "If you must know, I wasn't the best looking guy in high school."

"You're cute now," she said, and smiled .

"Don't patronize me," he said, his tone amused. "Back then I spent a lot of time in the friendzone. It wasn't fun, but it provided me the unique position to see what happened to girls when guys were tools.

They would come to me and share their stories and I decided I never wanted to make a girl feel such heartache."

She laughed sourly. "I know heartache far too well."

"Old boyfriend?"

"Jason," she admitted.

"How long were you together?"

"Two years, since our senior year of high school," she admitted. "He followed me to the University of Colorado."

"When did it end?" he asked.

"We broke up a year ago," she said, taking a bite of her sandwich. She fleetingly wondered why she was talking about it, but he'd asked. Hoping to end the conversation, she added, "I almost married him."

"What was he like?"

"You *want* to talk about my ex?"

He withdrew two bottles of lemonade, offering one to her. "Learning about him is learning about you."

"Clever," she said. "But I'm not sure I believe you."

He flashed his easy smile and motioned her to continue, so she did. Aside from the blondes, few knew the whole story. Not even her mother understood what had gone wrong, but Reed wasn't connected to anyone, giving her a surprising sense of freedom.

She shared when they'd met in high school, how they'd dated through graduation and into college. He was academic but enjoyed sports and soccer. Their shared love of the outdoors had been a factor in their choice of college, but they'd hardly ever gone to the mountains.

Their first date became every date. Dinner on Friday night, followed by a movie. Visiting his family on the weekends, and a few holidays with her family when they could get to Arizona. It was comfortable and easy, but that was all it was. She finished her story with the fateful Valentine's Day when she'd turned him down.

23

"Why'd you do it?" he asked.

Others had asked the question, but the way he asked it, without judgment, without condemnation, brought the truth from her lips.

"I don't know."

He raised an eyebrow. "Really?"

She shrugged, her eyes on the stunning vista. "I thought I loved him, but I guess I was wrong."

"Love is more than just an emotion," he said. "It's wanting to be with someone."

"I *did* want to be with him," she said, a touch of heat creeping into her voice.

He shrugged and bent to the cooler, casting over his shoulder. "I suspect you didn't."

"What are you, the love Yoda?" she asked.

He grinned and held up two cookies. "Chocolate chip or macadamia nut?"

"Do you know the answer?"

His grin widened and he gave her the Macadamia nut, eliciting a laugh. As she finished her sandwich and ate the cookie—which was still warm—she thought about Jason, for the first time realizing that at some point their relationship had just become . . . comfortable. No spark, no fun, just comfortable. She voiced the thought and he nodded.

"So you're saying he was an old pair of sweat pants?"

"There's nothing wrong with sweat pants," she said defensively. "They're really comfortable."

"True," he said. "But who wants to spend their life in them?"

She snorted. "If I ever do, it means I've given up hope."

He chuckled and began to package up the wrappers, returning everything to the cooler. When he finished, Kate half expected him to scoot closer on the log, but instead he remained at a discreet distance.

"Do you really call your roommates the blondes?" he asked.

She burst into a laugh. "*That's* what you got from my story?"

"Your hair may be brown, but it's got some blonde as well—a pretty gold in this light."

She smiled at the offhand compliment. "Two years ago my roommates dressed up as blonde celebrities for a Halloween party at a club. Some guy mistook them for waitresses. When Brittney said she wasn't, he said they were just dumb blondes and they should get him a drink or go back to the kitchen. Ember kicked him in the groin."

Reed winced. "Really?"

Kate smiled as she recalled hearing the story. "Ember stood over him as he whimpered on the floor and said, 'the blondes would eat you for breakfast.' The name stuck."

"I would have liked to see that," he said. "But it's starting to get cold. Ready for the next activity?"

She cast a final look at the setting sun, wondering how she could be so cold yet feel so warm. Reluctantly she nodded and stood, but he reached into his pocket and pulled out his phone, pointing her to turn around.

"Ember was insistent she get a picture of the date," he said, his tone apologetic. "Do you mind?"

"She wanted proof of life?"

"Something like that," Reed said, standing with her so the selfie would show the view. "She didn't want you to skip out on the date."

"She's going to make a fearsome mother someday," Kate said, smiling for the picture.

He clicked it and showed her the image. Their smiles were frozen in time, the sun descending below the horizon over her shoulder, the light playing off her cheek. She found herself examining his features, pleased with the scruff on his chin and the glint of amusement in his eyes.

They gathered their things and followed the trail back to the car. As he continued the game from earlier she considered how he'd listened to her story. He'd changed the subject at the end, but she got the impression he'd done it for her sake, not his.

When they left the mountains behind, she shifted in her seat to examine him anew. He noticed her expression and his lips twitched, but he continued to wait. Then he smiled and raised an eyebrow.

"Is that the look you give an engineering problem?"

"Yes," she said.

"What do you want to know?" he asked.

"I've never met anyone like you. It's like you're a . . .," she struggled for the right word, "professional dater."

He laughed as he flipped on the headlights and pulled out of the canyon. "That wasn't a question."

"Are you a virgin?"

He burst into a laugh. "A bold question for a blind date."

"No one plans this much for a date—without an expectation."

"I *do* have an expectation," he said, and then grinned. "I expect you to enjoy yourself."

"You plan this much so I can have fun?"

Their eyes met. "Why not? Don't you deserve it?"

She snorted but had no answer to that, and for several moments they rode in silence. Intrigued and confused, she tried to imagine what had made Reed date in such a manner. Then his easy smile returned and he glanced her way.

"If you must know," he said. "I am a virgin."

She hadn't really expected an answer to the question, but he provided it with an amused expression. She sensed that he was being truthful, and he answered without fear of judgment or scorn. She guessed he had no qualms about admitting it, even if he were placed in a room of other guys. They might deride him for it, but he wouldn't care.

At the same time there was a strange reserve for one so open, as if he had more he chose not to share. He'd said what drove him to date as he did, but she guessed there was more to the story, parts he didn't share on a first date. Or perhaps at all.

But what did he keep hidden? Had he loved and lost? Or was he too afraid of love to let himself fall? She wanted to ask if he'd ever had a girlfriend but wasn't certain she wanted to keep pushing him. Short of using handcuffs, she'd treated him like a suspect in a murder investigation. Still, she wanted answers.

"Ready for the first activity?" he asked.

"Do you have some sort of manual you're following?"

"You know, you're the first to ask that."

"Do you?"

"Usually I follow a certain order," he said. "A creative dinner, an activity or two, and then the after-date dessert."

"Tell me one of your favorites."

He consented with a nod. "I was visiting some friends in Florida and took a girl to see the bioluminescent algae. The entire ocean glows in iridescent green and blue, lighting up with the passage of boats. One of the greatest things I've ever seen."

"Are you trying to win a gold medal in dating?"

"Maybe."

She grinned in resignation. "What's our next activity?"

He pulled off the road into a parking lot, where he exited and came around to open her door. She stood to find that they had come to a park. Lit by towering lights, the park contained a hill at its center. Snow blanketed the northern slope while the southern exposure showed withered grass.

He stepped to the trunk and withdrew a partially inflated raft, like the kind you would pull behind a boat. Dragging it behind them, he added air on his way toward the green side of the hill. When she realized what he intended she balked.

"I'm not dressed for sledding."

"We aren't sledding," he replied, "we're downhill boating."

"I'm wearing sneakers!" she protested.

"Hence the boat," he replied, his eyes twinkling like blue sapphires. "Trust me."

Both breathing hard, they reached the top of the slope and looked down the snowy side of the hill. Several runs had been carved in the snow but one stood out. Wide and smooth, it swept down the embankment and extended until it died in the grass.

"My roommate and I like to snowboard," Reed said. "And we sometimes come here when we don't have time to hit a resort. This year the kids from the school decided to make a tube run and cover it with water to make it faster."

"I don't even have a hat," she said.

He grinned and positioned the boat. "Grass at the beginning and end," he said. "So the question is, how fast do you want to go?" He offered his hand.

Time seemed to halt as she looked at him, his easy smile an invitation. In the last vestiges of light his black hair seemed to glisten, excitement lighting his eyes. Heat stirred into her chest. On instinct she sought to stifle it, extinguishing it before it could take root. But it refused to die. Instead it spread into a smile.

And she took his hand.

Chapter 5

"It's been years," she said, climbing into the boat.

"I figured," he replied, and then jumped in after.

She grabbed the ropes on the sides of the boat as they accelerated, the now frigid air blasting her face and hair as they careened down the hill. The ice had melted a little during the day, making the run even faster.

A spontaneous shout was drawn from her lips as the boat accelerated. Then they reached the bottom of the hill and the boat streaked into the field, bouncing and spinning. It passed over the grass and slowed dramatically, sending them both tumbling into the front. Laughing in delight, they disentangled themselves and exited the boat.

"Care for another run?" he asked.

The adult in her wanted to shake her head and argue, but the kid would not be restrained. She giggled and caught the rope. When was the last time she'd giggled? Then she pulled it around the hill and they began to climb.

When they plummeted down the slope she closed her eyes for a moment and relished the sensation of speed. Exhilarating and unnerving, it seemed to free her from the shackles that had bound her for a year. The sheer movement after being stuck for so long was almost addictive, and she veritably skipped up the hill for a third run.

She wiggled her way out at the bottom, eager to go again, even higher than before. He followed suit and they climbed up the hill, heaving the boat and leaping at the same time to gain a tiny boost of acceleration. She laughed the whole way down, shedding another layer of stifling regret.

After several runs fatigue drove them to slow, and they talked and laughed as they struggled up the green slope. She realized it had been nearly a decade since she'd gone sledding, and he admitted it had been a while as well. She tried to kick the mud off her shoes but he shook his head.

"Don't bother unless you want to stop."

"Never," she said fervently.

He grinned and helped her the last few steps. Then they retreated and sprinted toward the summit. Kate jumped high and twisted, landing in the boat with Reed at her side. The impact sent them slightly off course and they hit a jump, briefly soaring into the air before landing on the snow again. Her laugh filled the park as they spun their way to a stop.

Gasping for breath, they remained in the boat, both staring at the sky. In the cold and stillness it began to snow, the flurries sprinkling upon them, shimmering and gleaming in the street lights. She reached up in wonder and caught a snowflake.

"I didn't think it was going to snow tonight."

"The forecast said it might," he said.

"You checked the forecast?" she asked.

"Have to," he replied. "I was planning an outside date, after all."

She watched the snow descend from a sky that did not herald a storm. Instead it was the peace only wrought by a snowfall under the stars, when sound is stifled and solitude is welcomed. She'd felt alone for a year, but this time the solitude was not solitary.

"I never saw snow until I came here," she said softly.

"Really?" he asked.

She caught another snowflake. "I first saw snow my freshman year," she said. "I stood outside and let it drift onto my shoulders, stunned by the quiet and peace."

"I love the snow," he said, the smile evident in his tone. "It makes me want to curl up and read a book by the window."

She twisted her head to look at him. "What books?"

They talked books and movies, laughing as they quoted their favorites. Their taste in literature was largely shared, and they both loved Harry Potter. He'd read all the books but admitted having only seen the first few movies, a fact that drew no small amount of ire.

"Aren't you cold?" he finally asked.

She smiled. "I'm actually warm."

His eyebrows knit together as if he doubted her words. She met his gaze while flakes of snow floated around them, an endless vista of drifting white. She wondered if such magic permeated every date, but in that moment she didn't care.

"Tell me another fact," she said.

"I have a numb spot on my ankle," he said.

"How?"

"I cut my leg when I was a kid and the doctors said I nicked a nerve. It's about two inches long."

"I've broken five bones," she replied.

"At the same time?"

Her laughter was muffled by the snow. "Each a different accident, two by car, one by hammock, one by horse, and one by friend."

"Your friend broke your arm?" he asked.

"He didn't mean to," she said. "We were at a party and he was drinking and tripped on a step. He went down and knocked me down the stairs."

"And you forgave him?"

"He wasn't a mean drunk," she said with a smile. "Just a clumsy one."

He laughed. "I don't drink."

"At all?"

"Nope," he replied. "Never have. My dad liked to and I didn't like what it did to him."

"You've told me about your sister but not your parents," she said.

Reed shrugged and told a story of his parents, who were also divorced. When Reed was sixteen his dad had left his phone home and she found a wealth of incriminating texts. He'd returned from work to find everything he owned on the lawn.

"Do you see him often?" she asked.

"Not anymore," he said. "He's dating a woman in Virginia and is more interested in her than me or my sister." He laughed sourly. "I'm sure that's how every divorce goes."

"Not my parents," Kate said. "One day they realized they were just friends, so they split up. They're still friends. I think they're even in a bowling league together."

He snorted. "I don't think that's normal."

"I agree," she said. "But their bowling team is really good."

He laughed. "I think if my parents went bowling she'd crush him with the ball."

She watched his expression as he talked about his parents but it didn't last long. He took the first opportunity to steer the conversation to lighter topics, and she got the impression he didn't usually talk about his family with his dates.

With the snow caressing their cheeks, they spoke of their time in school and their goals. The drifting snow settled into his black hair and she laughed and brushed it free. She recalled running her hands through Jason's hair, but the memory was no longer tinged with regret.

Reed's features were darkened by shadows, but the streetlights cast a dim glow on his form. He lay in the boat next to her—yet not against her. The spacing was no doubt intentional as he held to his inner rules. She wanted to scoot closer but suspected he would pull away. Despite the distance she felt an inexorable pull, and found in his eyes a sense of grounding she'd thought lost.

When he noticed her shivering he frowned and lifted her up. "Time to leave."

"Can we do one more run?" she pleaded.

He smiled. "As you wish."

Chapter 6

One run turned into ten, and for the next hour they boated down the snow. At one point they briefly did battle, throwing snowballs at each other with unbridled fury until laughter overcame them. She would have stayed all night, but the dropping temperature finally drove them from the park. Breathless and elated, she reluctantly sprinted to the car.

Shivering, she sat in the car waiting for the heat to warm her skin, but the fan kept cutting out. Prepared for the possibility, Reed pulled a blanket from the back seat and handed it to her. Kate wrapped herself in the cloth and cast a look at the hill while the car backed out of the lot. She watched the snowy slope until a building blocked it from view, wondering if she would ever again feel such a sense of freedom.

"This isn't really fair," Kate said, still shivering.

"What do you mean?" he asked, blowing warm breath onto his hands.

"You plan this date so it cannot be beaten," she said. "And from now on every other date will just be disappointing."

"It's not my fault other guys don't do this," he said, and jerked a thumb at the park.

"Seriously," she said, and then skewered him with a look. "How many girls have fallen in love with you just from one date?"

"Love is a strong word," he said. "And I've never said it to a girl before."

"More rules?" she asked with a laugh. She realized her hair was in disarray and raked her hands through it, trying to tame the mess. "But how many have said they loved you?" she pressed.

"Some have misconstrued my intentions in the past," he admitted.

His tone had gained a defensive note. Reed really did like to make a date happy, but didn't do it out of attraction or interest. Again, she sensed there was more from his past than he wasn't saying.

She was curious, but decided not to press the question, instead asking him about his coursework. He was easy to talk to and funny, and she found the conversation as delightful as the activities of the date.

"My brothers almost shot one of my boyfriends," she said.

His eyes widened. "Really?"

She grinned, recalling the memory. "He honked from the road and they 'happened' to be cleaning their guns at the time. They marched out to explain how I should be treated. He was understandably apologetic."

"And your brothers?"

"Two are military," she said. "One Air Force and going for Special Forces, the other went into the Marines, much to my father's irritation. The third decided he liked cars instead of boot camp."

"Should I be nervous?" he asked.

"Only if you mistreat me," she said.

He saluted. "I'll do my best."

The fan kicked on and she leaned into the sudden heat, grateful for the warmth. Shivering again, she let the heat blast her face until her limbs began to tingle with warmth. Then she noticed her shoes and pointed to the marks.

"Not every girl would have been willing to get their shoes dirty," she said.

"Ember said you like the outdoors," he said. "I figured it was worth the risk."

"It was worth it," she said. "But I'm not sure you can top the downhill boating."

"We'll see," he replied, his blue eyes sparkling as he turned onto campus and pulled onto a street leading up a hill.

"Is that the observatory?" she asked.

"Don't tell me you don't like the stars."

"But I expected something . . . more." She smiled to let him know she was teasing.

He grinned. "Watching the stars is perhaps a little cliché. But that's not why we're here."

He parked in the empty lot and stepped around the car to open her door. Then he led her up the stairs to the front entrance. To her surprise Reed produced a key and unlocked the door, allowing them entry. Locking it behind them, he guided her through the darkened offices to the theater at the back.

"My friend works here," he said. "And she said we could use it for tonight."

He entered the theater and made his way to a table set up at the back, where a thermos and several jars were placed in neat order. He pulled two mugs from the stack and poured steaming hot chocolate from the thermos.

"I'm allergic to chocolate."

"You and your roommates drink it by the gallon every fall," he said.

She laughed in chagrin. "You asked Marta if I drink hot chocolate?"

"Didn't have to," he replied. "She likes to talk, and the last few months you were a frequent topic of conversation. She'd tried to get me to take you out before, but my schedule was already full."

"You already knew about Jason," she suddenly realized.

"Guilty," he said, "but it was a skewed version." He then gestured to the jars lined up on the table. "You can add whatever you like. Personally, I suggest the junior mints, or perhaps the peanut butter, if you're feeling adventurous."

Reed added junior mints and a candy cane, and then put a handful of Oreos and mint fudge cookies onto a napkin. Uncertain what to make of his knowledge regarding Jason, she dropped the junior mints into her cup and added a mountain of miniature marshmallows. Then she grabbed her own cookies and followed him to the back seats of the theater.

Finally settling on irritation, she said, "You knew about Jason and let me talk anyway."

"I'm not sure how much I knew," Reed said, taking a seat. "Coming from her, the story was tinged with a shocking amount of hatred. The blondes are certainly loyal."

She couldn't help but smile at his use of the nickname. She sipped on the hot chocolate and then nibbled on her cookie. His smile was now apologetic, and she couldn't hold onto her irritation.

"The after-date dessert is good," she said, and meant it. The drink was delicious and warm after the snow, and she relished the sensation of heat spreading throughout her body.

He pulled a remote into view and aimed it toward the projector booth. "I hope you like Looney Toons."

The familiar Bugs Bunny appeared on the enormous curved screen, the distinct WB introduction coming through the speakers. Delighted with the choice in video, she sipped her hot chocolate for several minutes and just enjoyed the moment. Then she threw him a look.

"This is usually when the guy would try to kiss me."

"Rest easy," he said without taking his eyes from the ceiling. "I told you my rules."

"What if your date tries to kiss you?"

"Shh," he said. "I love Marvin the Martian."

She smiled and returned her attention to the hot chocolate. The episode was childish but amusing, and gave a sense of nostalgia that reminded her of childhood. Even if she tried, she could not stop the smile on her face.

Part of her wanted to embrace the attraction she felt for Reed, but his behavior made it abundantly clear that he dated a lot. As she watched the cartoons she found herself wondering about the other girls and fighting jealousy. Then she frowned and reminded herself that Reed had pulled her from her haze of regret, and that was likely the source of her attraction. That's all it was. But even in her mind it sounded like a lie.

Chapter 7

They watched one episode and then another. When the third finished Reed checked his watch and sighed. He turned off the projector, and the lights returned to the image of the stars. Then he rose and gathered the supplies, putting everything into a box that had been underneath the table. She helped gather it and then looked to him.

"Just how long did it take to set this up?"

"A couple of hours," he replied as they walked to the door.

"Is that normal?"

He grunted in amusement. "You are the most curious date I've ever had."

"You invest time into a girl you don't even know," she said. "And I still wonder why."

"Did you have fun?"

"Best date I've ever had," she said.

"Then it was worth it," he said.

They walked to the car together and he popped the trunk to put the box inside the partially deflated boat. Then he stepped to her door and unlocked it, swinging it open for her. Their eyes connected as he stepped to the side, and she was surprised to find him even more attractive than when he'd appeared on her doorstep.

Their eyes met and she marveled at the blue. The snow was still descending, and it had again settled into his hair. His smile was earnest and light, and he didn't flinch from the proximity. He held the door for her, an act few guys had ever done, yet did so with the ease of familiarity.

She instinctively drifted closer to him and tilted her chin upward, a universal invitation. Attraction flickered in Reed's eyes before his features tightened and he withdrew. The sting was sudden but brief, and she forced an awkward laugh, using the moment to slip into the car.

Reed shut her door and strode around the car to get into the driver's seat. After a moment of silence their conversation resumed on the way back to her house, but inwardly she considered her action, wondering at his response. He'd warned her, but she'd never quite believed him.

"In by midnight," he said as he put the car in park.

"Another rule?"

"One I try to stick to," he said. "But for practical reasons. I still have work and school."

He came around the car and opened her door, walking her to her door. After the moment at the observatory she wasn't certain what to expect, but he smiled and offered a hug, which she gladly returned. When they parted she began to laugh.

"The bar has been set," she said.

"Then my work is complete," he said. "Goodnight Kate. I had fun tonight."

He pretended to tip an imaginary hat and then left. He climbed into his Camry and it coughed to life, and she turned and swung the door open, stepping into the familiar warmth of her house. Like lions to prey, the blondes pounced.

"How was it?"

"You weren't out very late."

"Did he kiss you?"

Kate's smile returned, and for the first time she noticed a spot of chocolate on her coat. Wiping it with her finger, she stared at the smudge while her roommates' questions became more ardent. She didn't answer because she didn't know how to, but for some reason she thought of the story she'd shared when she'd jumped into the river.

"Well?" Ember demanded, "What was it like?"

Kate finally met their eyes. "Like falling," she murmured. "Only I think this time I liked the impact." They stared at her in confusion, but her smile only widened.

They demanded answers and Kate dished, wanting to cement the night into memory before it could fade. Her roommates gave the appropriate praise and shock to each event, with all three displaying matching expressions of wonder.

"But you weren't dressed for the snow!" Ember exclaimed.

Kate laughed and proceeded with the telling, relishing the attention from her captive audience. With a start she realized it was the first time in a year she'd sat with her roommates and just talked.

Brittney darted to the kitchen and returned with two plates of cookies, one her famous white chocolate macadamia nut, the second her double chocolate fudge. She offered both plates to Kate.

"Chocolate for a terrible Valentine's Day," she said. "Or your favorite if you had a good night."

Kate grinned and picked up a white chocolate macadamia nut, drawing crows of delight from the girls. Kate couldn't suppress the smirk as she bit into the cookie and savored the distinct flavors.

"Are you going out again?" Ember asked.

Kate almost said yes but hesitated. She wanted to—a great deal actually—and not just because the date was fun. Reed was interesting and honorable. And there was clearly more to him that begged to be discovered.

She could not deny the attraction she felt towards him, and took a moment to try and explain it away. But the harder she told herself it was just Reed being nice, the more she wanted to see his smile again. But would *he* want to date *her*?

She'd seen attraction in Reed's eyes when she'd given the opportunity for a kiss, an undeniable desire to reach for her. Still, she suspected it was not enough for him to ask her out on a second date. He'd made it clear he didn't date exclusively. Then she had an idea.

"We'll go out again," she said firmly.

"When?" Marta asked, eager for details.

Kate's smile turned sly. "When I ask him."

Part 2: The Challenge Date

Chapter 8

Reed stared at the calendar on his wall. Packed with classes, work, and other activities, it also tracked his upcoming dates. It was the middle of the semester and he had a good idea of the school workload, but his research class was brutal, with more homework than the other two combined.

He tapped his pencil on his desk, considering whom he'd set up for his date next Saturday. Sara was an old friend, one he'd taken on several dates. They were in the same program and frequently studied for exams together. She was fun and flirty and whenever he had a free night he took her out. The following week was Melissa, a girl he'd met in the library. Two weeks after that was Jill, a recent graduate and a friend of a friend. She didn't yet know his rules.

He didn't kiss or hold hands unless he wanted to date exclusively. The rule came as a surprise to most of his dates, especially girls that were used to guys wanting much more. But for him the rule was essential, allowing him to avoid the inevitable complications that came with sex. He'd also been raised to believe that sex should be reserved for marriage. He recognized that the current culture viewed the notion as archaic, but he found the prospect appealing.

As he looked across his calendar his eyes were drawn to a day two weeks ago, Valentine's Day. Blind dates were not uncommon for him, and many of his friends or former dates liked to set him up. But this had been different, and Kate lingered on his mind.

She was beautiful and clever, but she harbored a subtle courage he found appealing. She'd grilled him like a veteran police officer, her skeptical smile only serving to make her more attractive. She'd revealed a great deal about herself, but he wanted to know more, and normally when he enjoyed a date so much he asked the girl out again. This time he hadn't for a simple reason.

She made him nervous.

Jackson appeared in his door and leaned against the frame while he ate his standard dinner, a bowl of cereal. Tall and athletic, Jackson played soccer, basketball, lacrosse, and pretty much any sport he could find. His girlfriend was just as competitive as he was, leading to both fun and fighting between them.

"Who are you going with this week?" Jackson asked.

"Sara on Friday."

Jackson began to speak, nearly spilling milk down his chin. "Why don't you call Kate back? We both know you like her."

"And what makes you think that?" Reed asked with a smile.

"Because you haven't called her."

Reed swept his hands wide. "And that means I like her?"

"You're afraid of her."

Stung, he frowned. "You think I'm afraid? I date three times a week. I'm not afraid."

"Then call her," he said.

Reed picked up his phone and made to dial Kate's number but hesitated, his finger on send. Jackson issued a triumphant laugh and turned away, returning to the kitchen to refill his bowl. Reed stared at his phone like it was a foreign object. With a sigh he looked at the calendar, to the 14th of February, Valentine's Day.

Reed was a teacher's assistant when he'd met Kate's roommate, Marta. She'd heard of Reed's dating habits, and approached him to go out with Kate. She'd been insistent that it be Valentine's Day, which he usually took off from his dating hobby. But Marta had proved impossible to refuse.

"Are you a virgin?" Kate had asked halfway through the date.

He smiled, recalling her expression, the hint of a smile, the sparkle of suspicion in her eyes. She'd suspected him to be dishonest at first,

45

thinking his words a ploy to seduce her. But he adhered to his first rule with absolute regard—even when she'd almost kissed him. Others had tried to, but with Kate it had been different. He'd *wanted* to kiss her.

He stared at her name on the calendar, the four letters scrawled in his nearly illegible handwriting. He recalled the date in his mind, trying to convince himself that he'd merely gotten caught up in the magic he'd been trying to create. But if that was true, why did she make him nervous?

Realizing Jackson was right, he released a sigh and sank into the chair at his desk. He was attracted to Kate, and that very reason stopped him from asking her out again. Shaking himself, he turned to the next few days, determined to cast Kate from his mind.

The doorbell rang and he leaned back to see who was there. The house they lived in was small and contained two bedrooms, each facing the living room. Adjacent to the living room was the kitchen and a bathroom on opposite sides. From his bedroom he saw Jackson open the door, still with his bowl of cereal in hand.

"Is Reed here?"

"Come in," Jackson said, waving vaguely toward the bedroom and then raising his voice. "It's for you!"

Reed put down his pencil and left his room, stepping into the living room to greet the girl. It took a moment before he recognized her as Kate's roommate, Ember. Slim and short, she had fiery red hair and an intimidating gaze.

"Ember, right?"

The girl smiled, revealing gratitude that he'd remembered her name. But her expression bore a touch of mischief as well. She reached into her pocket and withdrew an envelope which she handed to him.

"What's this?" he asked.

"An invitation."

"An invitation for what?"

"How does it feel to be the one in the dark?" Ember said. She smirked and left, laughing as she shut the door.

Jackson poked his head into the living room. "What just happened?"

"I'm not sure," Reed replied, opening the envelope.

He unfolded the paper to find an invitation. A slow smile spread on his face as he read it, and then reread it. In all his dating, he'd never once had a girl ask *him* on a date, and the prospect sent a thrill of excitement through his chest.

Reed Hansen

You are invited to a night in the past. Attire is semi-formal and your arrival is expected promptly at 6:00. Dance shoes are recommended.

Kate

On the back of the card was an address for a location downtown. He frowned, trying to recall what was there. Aside from a few gas stations and warehouses, the area was not the usual date destination.

"You'd better get ready," Jackson said. "You've only got thirty minutes."

Reed turned to find Jackson's expression now smug. "You knew about this?"

"It's possible a certain lady asked for my assistance," he replied. "And who am I to resist?"

Reed leveled the paper at him in accusation. "You told me to keep tonight free so I could help you with your homework."

"I did?" Jackson screwed up his face in mock confusion. "I must have gotten the nights wrong. I have a game with Shelby tonight."

"Traitor," Reed said.

Jackson smirked and used his spoon to point at Reed's door. "I'd suggest you wear a button up and a vest."

"You know what I'm doing," he realized.

"I know nothing," he said with a sniff. "You'd better get going."

Reed plied him for answers, but Jackson merely ate his cereal with a smile on his face. Realizing he didn't have time to wait for an answer, Reed hurried to his room. Then he looked at the invitation again, the words eliciting a thread of excitement. He had no idea what Kate had planned, and he wondered if this is what his dates might feel.

He dressed in black slacks, a vest, and the dance shoes he'd picked up for a date a few months ago. Then he cinched a red tie and stepped into the living room. Shelby had arrived while he was getting ready and she whistled at his appearance.

"Who's your date this time?"

Nearly as tall as Jackson, Shelby was dressed in basketball shorts and a jersey for their intramural team. With brown hair and brown eyes, she was attractive and forceful, a combination that appealed to Jackson from the moment he'd met her—the night Reed had taken her out.

Jackson laughed as he laced his basketball sneakers. "She asked *him*."

"Oh?" she asked, her eyes sparkling with sudden interest. "Do tell."

"Later," Jackson said, standing up to kiss her. "Our game starts in an hour."

"We'll be here when you get back," she said to Reed. "I expect full details."

"I'll dish like a teenage girl," Reed said, causing them both to laugh.

Reed grinned and picked up his keys. Slipping out the door, he strode to his Camry and coaxed it to life. Then he pulled out of his parking spot and drove to the highway, taking the exit to downtown Boulder.

The GPS on his phone brought him to a section of the city south of downtown. Just as he remembered, the place was nearly empty, with warehouses interspersed with the occasional gas station or market.

He found the address and pulled into a packed parking lot. At odds with the area, the people standing outside the building were equally as dressed up, with suits and vintage dresses in abundance.

He didn't bother locking his car and strode to the entrance, threading his way through the older couples. The music wafting from the interior came from a different era, and he paused to examine the sign above the door.

The Big Band Ballroom

Intrigued, he passed an older couple and swung the door open, finding himself in a ballroom straight out of the 1950s. A full jazz band played on a stage while a collection of older couples danced with surprising vigor and style.

Grey-haired women rotated on the dance floor, their dresses twirling and spinning. Men in suits and ties caught their hands and lead, their feet skipping across the floor, never missing a beat.

Mirrors on the walls made the repurposed warehouse seem gigantic, and reflected the muted lighting to set a romantic atmosphere. Aged pictures hung from the non-mirrored walls, their black and white prints depicting dancing couples.

Then the woman singing on the stage spotted him and swept a hand to the band, cutting them off. The dancers on the floor came to a stop and applauded, but she waved for silence, and once the noise dimmed she pointed to Reed at the door.

"We have a new guest with us tonight," she said, a smile spreading on her wrinkled face. "Reed, I presume? You're right on time."

All eyes turned to Reed, the shorter couples craning to get a look at him. One man cursed when his view was blocked, and his wife shushed him. Reed smiled and offered a short bow, and then swept his hands at the gathering of dancers.

"Can anyone point me in the direction of my date?" he asked.

"She's already on the dance floor," the elderly woman at the microphone replied.

She pointed to the bass player and he began to pluck the strings, setting a slow and inviting tone. The sax player joined in, and a moment later the rest of the band added their music. The couples began to dance and spin, their motions parting the way for Reed to spot a figure standing at the center of the ballroom.

Wearing a flowing red dress, Kate smiled when their eyes met. He'd thought her beautiful before, but this time she took his breath away. Her dark hair was tied back with a ribbon that matched her dress, her shoes sparkling and sleek.

He grinned and made his way to her, weaving between couples dancing swing like they were in their twenties. Several of the men were old enough to be Reed's grandfather, and they winked and gave knowing nods.

"Go get her, tiger," one said.

Reed grinned. "I'll see what I can do."

He reached Kate and she offered her hand. "I'm guessing you know how to dance," she said.

"A fair assumption," he replied.

"Then may I have this dance?"

"Doesn't the guy do the asking?"

"Not this time," she said, her smile positively wicked. "This time I'm in charge."

He took her hand. "Do I get to lead?"

Kate's green eyes sparkled. "I'll allow it," she said. "But only if you can sweep me off my feet . . ."

Chapter 9

Reed pulled her into a twirl and then set them into a basic swing. It had been some time since he'd taken a girl dancing, but he remembered enough to impress. What came as a surprise was her skill.

"Where'd you learn to dance?" he asked. "Most girls don't know how to swing dance."

She came out of a spin and wrapped her arm around him. "Here."

"Really?" he asked. "When?"

"The last two weeks."

He realized what she meant and raised an eyebrow. "When did you start planning this date?"

"February fourteenth," she admitted. "At midnight. After you dropped me off. I wanted a second date but suspected you would have a full schedule, so I planned my own."

"And Jackson?"

Her smile turned smug. "He was quite the willing accomplice."

Reed pulled her into a spin and caught her back, dropping her into a dip. "How very devious of you," he said.

She grinned, the expression betraying her nervousness. On the last date Kate had been reserved and suspicious, but apparently that was just a circumstance of her life. She'd opened up on the date, but he'd never imagined she could be so bold.

She'd thought of him a great deal in the last two weeks, planning a date and dancing to prepare. The knowledge that he'd been on her thoughts sent a thrill into his chest, the emotion heightened by the necessary contact of the dance.

"Have you ever asked a guy out?" he asked, pulling up from the dip.

"Never," she said breathlessly.

"You're a natural," he teased. "And using my roommate against me was a masterful stroke."

"I thought it was quite ingenious," she said. "But it makes me wonder, how many more of your friends would be as willing to betray you . . ."

"Just how many dates do you have planned for me?" he asked.

"None," she said, and rotated close enough to kiss. "Yet."

He spun her out and laughed again, pleased by her response. And for several minutes they just danced, every turn offering a new vantage point to examine her profile. Their skill fell woefully short of the geriatric dancers around them, leading to many false starts and stumbles, but the mistakes prompted as much laughter as the flawless turns.

"Are there any other talents I should know about?" he asked.

She sniffed. "They await discovery."

The comment was a tease, suggesting more time together. Reed fleetingly realized that when they'd been apart he'd felt fear, but now that they were together he felt an entirely different emotion.

Desire.

The realization caused him to miss catching her hand and they collided. They both laughed. Then he caught her hand and spun her again, pulling her into a more complicated maneuver, which failed spectacularly.

"I hope you don't mind me taking a few pages from your handbook," she said.

He caught her hands as they began anew. "Which ones?"

The music began to speed up, making conversation difficult as they twirled. For the first time she showed her inexperience, but gamely sought to follow his lead through the faster steps. She laughed at her stumbles but did not request a reprieve.

"Dinner, an activity, followed by a dessert," she said.

"Did I miss dinner?" he asked, feigning alarm.

"You did," she said, laughing as he ducked under her arm and paused on the beat, and then pulled her back in. "But don't worry, I think you'll like the rest of the evening."

"What makes you say that?" he asked, catching her about the waist and pulling her close.

Startled, she squeaked in response, but he controlled her momentum and held her fast. The music ended and they stood inches apart, both breathing hard from the dance. He stared into her green eyes and, for an instant, did not retreat.

"You'll just have to trust me," she said.

Although he knew he should spin her away, he couldn't resist the impulse to linger. Her arm was draped on his neck, their hands intertwined. The proximity necessitated by the dance bent his rules without breaking them outright.

"Same rules?" he asked. He shifted backward a step, making it clear what he meant.

"Same rules," she said, and then smiled. "When you decide you want to date me exclusively, I'll *let* you kiss me."

He laughed and finally retreated, both from her and the spark of hope that kindled in his chest. As they separated he became aware of the scrutiny from the couples in the ballroom, many of which were dancing slow, their eyes on Reed and Kate. When they did not kiss there was an audible groan.

"Don't miss a chance to kiss a pretty girl, sonny," the nearest man said.

"That's how he got me," his wrinkled wife said.

"I'll remember that," Reed said.

Catching Kate's hand, he guided her toward the front of the ballroom, where an alcove allowed weary dancers a place of reprieve. Momentarily empty, the alcove also contained a drinking fountain. They each drank and then sat on the bench.

Latticework arced above the bench, the wood containing twinkling lights that flickered like streetlamps on a foggy night. Pictures of dancers from a different age hung on the walls while an old saxophone hung between them.

"Where did you find this place?" Reed asked, gesturing to the ballroom in wonder.

"I thought you'd already know of it," she said, clearly pleased she had managed to surprise him.

"Boulder's a big city," he replied. "But I'm still surprised I didn't know about a fifties dance hall."

"Brittney's grandmother likes to come here," she admitted. "My roommates and I schemed for hours until we came up with this idea. I knew how to dance but not like this, so I came for the daily lessons."

"Without a partner?"

She swept a hand at the room. "I had plenty of partners. Once they realized what I was up to, they were more than happy to help. Charles gets a little handsy, though."

She pointed at an older gentleman sporting a tie as wide as his head. He lacked a wedding ring and seemed to rotate through the other single women, his hand always sliding to his partner's rump.

"You should have slapped him," he said.

"I did."

He raised an eyebrow. "You actually slapped an old man?"

She flushed. "It was a reflex. I didn't hit him that hard."

54

"It doesn't look like he learned his lesson," he said, smothering a laugh as he saw Charles drift his hand down.

Kate grinned and motioned to the others. "Mrs. Wilson is the one in black and red. She taught me footwork. She smells like peaches, which she cans for sale at the farmer's market."

"There's a farmer's market?"

"On Seventh," she replied. "And the peaches are fantastic." She pointed to another couple. "Mary was my favorite. She witnessed me slapping Charles."

"What did she say?"

Kate grinned, her eyes sparkling at the memory. "Charles protested, but Mary said it served him right, that even children know to keep their hands to themselves."

"You braved handsy old men and peaches to prepare a date for me?"

"Has a girl asked you before?"

Reed shook his head. "Never. Once they learned what I did, they always wanted me to take them out."

Her expression was pleased, and he realized she'd wanted to be the first. She'd been conveying a confident air since his arrival, but now he spotted an undercurrent of nervousness in her expression. To ask him on a date—and attempt to best him—was a leap outside her comfort zone.

"You're setting the bar pretty high," he said.

She turned to him and raised an eyebrow. "I've never put this much into a date before," she admitted. "It's more difficult than I thought—but also tremendous fun."

"Why?"

She considered his question. "Your expression when you walked in the door, of excitement and awe, was worth every moment."

"That's my favorite part," he said, "seeing a date realize how much fun the night is going to be, the surprise and excitement." He paused for a moment. "So, you spent two weeks practicing dancing," he said. "What else did you do?"

Her eyes narrowed. "You really expect me to tell you the rest of the date?"

Caught, he grinned. "It was worth a shot."

Their conversation was interrupted by a diminutive couple that stopped for a drink. Kate grabbed Reed and pulled him onto the dance floor, pretending not to hear as the hunched man began to speak.

"Did I tell you about my . . ."

As they stepped onto the dance floor she leaned over to him. "That was Mr. Barris," she said, her tone conspiratorial. "He will *not* stop talking. And once he gets going, he always finds a way to talk about his prostate cancer."

Reed snorted a laugh. "Really?"

She held his gaze. "In detail."

He laughed and pulled her to an open area, spinning her into a twist that brought them onto the beat. Laughing, she followed his lead into a different style of swing. For the next several minutes they danced to music from a different age, but he found his thoughts drifting to their previous date.

Kate had been reserved and suspicious, but over the course of the night she'd gradually opened up, revealing hints of an adventurous spirit. He wondered how much had been suppressed by her relationship with Jason. Or was it their breakup?

She, too, observed him, and it wasn't until fatigue drove them from the dance floor that he realized why. She was attracted to him, that much was obvious, but she was also hesitant to pursue him. Asking him on a date presented a game, a distraction from her life following her breakup with Jason. But did she want more from him?

Or was he just a distraction?

Chapter 10

"Don't miss another chance to kiss her," Mr. Barris called out as they left.

"Thanks, Mr. Barris," Reed said, grinning and waving at the man.

They stepped into the night and Reed breathed deep of the cold air, relishing it after the heat of the dance hall. She held her jacket in her hands, shivering as the night breeze pulled at her dress.

"Well?" she asked.

"Like I said," he replied, "you're setting the bar pretty high."

"Good," she said, flashing a smug smile. "You ready for what's next?"

"You know, I've never been on the receiving end of a date before," he said. "And the curiosity is killing me."

"Perfect," she said with a mischievous smile. "Why don't we take my car and we'll come back for yours later."

"Sounds good to me."

Her car proved to be a newer model Toyota, and was much cleaner than his. She all but giggled as she held the door for him, her action prompting a woman at the door to shout out to them.

"That's not how it's done!"

"I know, Mrs. Agnus," she called.

The leather seats were freezing on his back and he shivered. She donned her jacket as she came around the car and slipped into her seat, turning the heat on as they pulled out of the parking lot.

"I can't believe you remembered their names," Reed said.

"What do you mean?" she asked.

"You could have just showed up and learned to dance, but you took the time to remember their names."

"They reminded me of my grandparents," she replied. "My grandfather was a veteran and one of the smartest men I've ever known."

"When did he die?" he asked, hearing the regret in her tone.

"Two years ago," she said. "He and my nana actually taught me to dance when I was in high school. Now she lives with my father outside of Phoenix."

"My grandfather lives in a retirement home in Florida," he said. "But he acts like a kid in college. He goes on as many dates as I do, but with walkers and wheelchairs."

She laughed and turned into the parking lot of a Walmart. He raised an eyebrow at the location but she merely smiled and pulled into a spot close to the door. She warned him to stay in his seat and came around to open the door for him, an act which made him grateful for the warmth in the car.

It was after 10:00 and the store was quiet, but she led him to the cookie aisle. Then she withdrew a strip of cloth and tied it around his head, blocking his vision. He grinned as he realized her intent.

"Am I supposed to pick one without knowing what it is?"

He heard the smile in her voice. "My brothers used to argue for hours over what treat to buy, so my parents decided to cover our eyes and give us ten seconds or we got nothing. I didn't always like the treat, but it was always an adventure."

"So I'm just supposed to reach out and choose one?"

"Not yet," she said.

She caught his arm and began to turn him, while moving him up and down the aisle with the spin. When he started to get dizzy he protested and she released him. He'd marked the location of the Oreos before the blindfold, but now had no idea.

"First one you touch is our treat," she said.

"I don't like how good you are at this," he said.

She laughed, the sound grateful and delighted. "Ten, nine, eight . . ."

He shifted his feet forward, reluctant to trip and fall into the shelves. Reaching out, he moved his hand up and down, left and right, until realizing it really didn't matter. He reached out and fumbled for a package. As he pulled back the blindfold he found mint fudge cookies in his hand.

"Hope you like mint," he said. "But I supposed you put mints into your hot chocolate."

"Good memory," she said, obviously pleased. "Now for the drink."

At his insistence, she donned the blindfold and picked their drink, which turned out to be orange soda. Then they finished at the cracker aisle, this time ending up with vinegar and sea salt potato chips. As they walked to the front of the store they laughed about their selection, and the strange looks they got from the store worker that rang them up.

"You really are clever at this," he said as they exited the store. "Did you do anything like this for other guys?"

She cocked her head to the side, her smile fading. Confused by her sudden shift in mood, he considered the response. Then she realized her thoughts had turned to Jason and tried to smooth the moment with a laugh.

"You'd better be careful," he said. "Or someone might fall for you."

She smiled at that, but it was a little forced. "You never said how many have fallen for you."

"Five have said the word love," he replied. "But I think more would have said it. You have to be careful when you use this superpower."

She snorted, the shadow in her eyes disappearing. "Is that what dating is, a superpower?"

He swept his hands at the dark parking lot. "What else would it be? You have the power to make someone else happy, to bring a smile to their face, a moment of joy in their overworked life."

"It sounds like a superpower when you put it that way," she said. "But if dating makes others happy, what makes *you* happy?"

"Isn't it obvious?" he asked. "Seeing a girl smile."

She grunted her doubt. "I suspect there is something more you want. You may have been honest with me, but you haven't revealed everything."

They were back in the car driving south, headed towards campus. His smile faded as he thought of her question. He'd thought he understood her, but she kept surprising him. Most of his dates were content to enjoy his efforts, and very few had wanted to know him.

"Dating is just . . . fun," he said with a shrug.

"Dating is drama," she corrected.

He laughed. "I don't think it has to be, not if you do it right."

"So I've been doing it wrong?" she asked, her smile making it clear she wasn't offended.

"I'm sorry," he said. "I don't mean to sound pretentious."

"You don't," she said. "But now you've got me curious."

He considered his next words, not wanting to say something else that sounded arrogant. "Perhaps it's not whether you are dating the right way or the wrong way, it's a question of purpose."

"And your purpose is fun."

"Exactly," he said.

"Most men date for sex," she said pointedly. "Or they don't date at all—but they still want the sex."

"That's a pretty sad purpose," he said.

She grinned. "It's not much better than women. Do you know why they date a guy?"

"Depends on the guy," he said. "Looks, money, pity."

"Pity dates don't count."

He laughed. "I had my share of those in high school."

"So you don't know what girls want?"

"I didn't say that," he replied. "I just don't want to sound pretentious again."

"I promise I won't think that," she said.

They exchanged an amused look, and he noticed her relaxed posture, her smile still a shade tentative. She was enjoying herself, but still held herself in reserve. He wondered if she'd asked him on a date because she considered him safe.

"Women want to matter," he said. "They want the guy to take them on a date and pay attention to them, think of them, to care."

"So it's the thought that counts?"

"Maybe," he said. "When I picked you up for our last date, I pretended I had no plans. What did you think?"

Her lips twitched in amusement. "I thought less of you."

"And what did you think when you realized I had actually planned a date."

She smiled. "That you were suddenly more attractive."

He gestured to her as if her comment made his point. "It's not the thought. It's how *much* thought."

"Do guys appreciate it as well?"

"Depends on the guy," he said. He realized they were headed towards the stadium. "Where exactly are we going?"

"You didn't tell me where we were going last time," she said. "So I'm following your rules."

"But why the stadium?"

"Does the professional dater not like being left in the dark?"

He grinned and shrugged. "Bring on the adventure."

Chapter 11

The stadium was located on a hill at the edge of campus. In the fall the parking lot filled with students, alumni, and crazed fans, and the scent of beer, grilled hot dogs, and processed nacho cheese filled the air. Although not a huge fan of football, Reed frequently went with Jackson and Shelby, who were the type to paint their faces and bodies in support of the team.

"Do you like football?" he asked as they pulled into the lot.

"I don't hate it," she said. "But I haven't enjoyed watching lately."

He heard the tone in her voice and raised an eyebrow. "Jason?"

She gave a sour expression. "I was hoping to make it through the night without talking about him."

Reed shrugged. "If you want to talk . . ."

"Not tonight," she said.

The look carried a trace of pleading, and he realized she really didn't want to discuss him. He acquiesced with a nod and she smiled her gratitude. Then she turned off the car and came around to open his door. Together, they walked to a side entrance of the stadium, where she regained a measure of her previous amusement.

"Can you climb?" she asked, motioning to the fence.

He hesitated, uneasy at the prospect of breaking into the school stadium. "I don't usually ask my dates to break laws when I take them out. Getting arrested is a real downer."

"Kidding," she said, and produced a key from her pocket. She unlocked the door and led them inside.

"How'd you get a key to the stadium?" he asked.

"You aren't the only one with connections."

Her smile flashed in the dim light as they crossed the room to another door, which led beneath the bleachers. Their footsteps echoed eerily off the stone and steel structure, the darkness adding to the sense of solitude.

"You're enjoying this entirely too much," he said.

"Being on this side is more fun than I thought," she admitted.

"I hope I didn't sound this condescending."

She burst into a laugh, the sound reverberating off the underside of the bleachers. "Planning the date was almost as much fun as the date itself."

"How much time did it take you?" he asked.

"Aside from the dancing, we spent most of last week hatching the rest of the plan," she said. "And the blondes proved adept at tactics."

"You make it sound like they're super villains."

"They are," she said fervently.

She led the way out from under the bleachers and onto the field, striding all the way to the fifty-yard line. Alone in the dark stadium, the moon and stars bathed them in soft light, illuminating a pile of blankets placed at the center of the field.

He pretended shock. "Just what do you expect out of the evening, my dear lady?"

"I want your cookies," she said, and took the sack from him with a laugh.

They settled onto the blanket and wrapped themselves against the chill. It was warm for early March, which meant the snow had melted, but it was still freezing. Wrapped in two quilts, Reed enjoyed the bite of the wind on his face.

She opened their treat and sampled the rather strange combination of mint fudge, vinegar chips, and orange soda. The starlight and stadium were a recipe for romance, and Reed stole surreptitious looks at his beautiful companion.

"There's one thing you didn't say that girls think about on a date," Kate asked.

"What's that?"

They were both on their backs, staring at the sky as it gradually rotated above. The stadium blocked the lights of Boulder, making the stars shine like crystals on dark velvet. He felt the desire to touch her hand, so he kept his fingers intertwined on his chest, safely beneath the blanket.

"Marriage."

"The big M," he said with a nod. "Do all women think about it?"

"Many," she said. "But not all."

"Do you even know what you want in a husband?" he asked.

"Do you know what you want in a wife?" she countered.

"Some of it," he replied. "I know I want her to have a sense of adventure, because life can be pretty dull without it."

"True," she said. "I want a guy who isn't afraid."

"Afraid?" he asked.

He rolled onto his side to see her and she did the same. "Guys act all tough, like nothing can scare them." she snorted in scorn. "But they're all terrified of the future."

"Like spaceships and science fiction?"

She grinned. "You know what I mean. Men are afraid of marriage, babies, fatherhood, changing diapers, growing old, and everything in between."

"You certainly know a great deal about us," he said.

"Most of the guys I've ever dated had zero interest in the future," she replied. "They were all afraid."

The shade of regret to her eyes suggested she was thinking of Jason, who'd proposed just a year ago. But if he'd proposed, what had he been afraid of? Reed thought he'd understood the story, but now realized there was more she'd left unsaid.

"And you're not afraid?" he asked.

"If I didn't care where I was going, it wouldn't matter what I do in the present."

"Are you quoting *Alice in Wonderland*?"

She smiled. "Doesn't mean it's not true."

"It's certainly true," he replied. "And so is your analysis of the average male psyche."

"Can you explain it to me?" she asked.

He smiled. "As an average male you would think I could explain the male mind—but sadly I cannot. Maybe it's the culture or maybe it's their parents."

"So how do I find a good one—oh master Yoda."

He laughed and reclined onto the blanket. "Same way I hope to find a good one. Keep dating until I find her."

She snorted. "That's easy for you to say. You get to do the asking."

"You can ask as easily as I can," he said, "and it appears you do quite well." Unwilling to pull his arms free of the blankets, he used his chin to point to the stadium.

"Really?" she asked, sweeping the dark bleachers with her eyes. "It's not too much?" Her tone was abruptly nervous.

He laughed. "Don't use this on just anyone. But if the guy is interested, it will certainly catch his attention."

"So you've met your match?" she pressed.

66

He sat up and looked at her. "What are you insinuating?"

"A game," she said, sitting up to meet his gaze.

With moonlight reflecting off her hair and sparkling in her eyes, she was stunningly beautiful, and the surge of attraction surprised him. He'd felt it on their first date and controlled it, but this time it was stronger, compelling him to lean closer.

He swallowed and held himself in check. Kate was beautiful, smart, and talented like many of those he'd asked out—but there was something intangible about her that commanded attention.

He fleetingly wondered if it was her willingness to ask him on a date, or perhaps her openness. The date she'd planned was as crafty as any he'd put together, and to be on the receiving end was more fun than he'd anticipated. Regardless of the reason, the prospect of more time with Kate instilled a yearning that could not be denied.

"What's the game?" he asked cautiously.

Her eyes sparkled. "It's more like a challenge than a game."

"I'm up for a challenge," he said warily. "As long as it doesn't get me arrested."

Her eyes glowed in the night. "Then I'm issuing a dating challenge."

Chapter 12

"You're throwing down a gauntlet?" he asked.

"Every two weeks," she said. "We take turns who does the asking, and we each try to top the other."

He laughed, surprised and intrigued. "You want to do a dating challenge . . . with me."

"Is the veteran is afraid of an upstart rookie?"

"Never," he said, and took a sip of his orange soda. The taste hit his tongue where he'd just eaten a cookie, and he grimaced.

She grinned at his expression. "Do you accept?"

"Just how many dates are you suggesting?" he asked, already planning what he would do for the next date.

She shrugged. "Does it matter? We quit whenever you concede defeat."

"That's not going to happen."

She sniffed, feigning disapproval. "I guess you're not up to the challenge."

"I never said that," he said. "Count me in. But who are the judges?"

"The blondes?"

"Too biased," he replied.

She snorted. "They would be more likely to support you than me. It took hours to get them on my side. For modern, progressive feminists, they're surprisingly traditional when it comes to dating."

"What does that mean?"

"They thought you should ask me out again."

He raised an eyebrow. "Why did you decide to ask me out?" It was the question that had burned since the moment he'd received the note from Ember, but he managed to keep his voice merely curious.

"The first date was fun," she said, suddenly hesitant. "And I didn't want to sit around waiting on you."

He noticed the evasive tinge to her tone and realized she wasn't revealing the whole truth. The juvenile part of him exulted in the prospect that she was more attracted to him than she let on, but he quashed it with the killer of passion, logic.

"This is one of the best dates I've ever had," he said sincerely. "You should consider a career change."

"Dating doesn't pay the bills," she lamented.

She shivered and wrapped the blanket tighter about her shoulders, the chill having finally breached the barrier. The relative heat from earlier had long since given way to the nightly chill. Both realized at the same time that it was getting late and set about cleaning up the blanket and desserts.

"Oh," she said. "We need to take a picture."

"Ember?"

She grunted in irritation. "All the blondes, actually. I swear they're like mother hens."

"It will make them happy," Reed said, and leaned in to the picture.

With moonlight lighting their faces and the stadium in the background, the picture showed the uprights over his shoulder. As the flash blinded him he sensed the beginning of a trend. He blinked to restore his vision and reached down to collect the things, but just as he picked up the folded blanket a faint click echoed in the stadium.

They both paused and looked at each other before scanning the dark recesses of the stadium. There was no sign of movement, only an odd rushing sound, like air being pushed by water down a tube . . .

"The sprinklers!" he shouted.

They bolted for the sideline as water shot into view, the sprinklers rising like vengeful rodents to spray water across the field. They dodged sprays, dancing across the field like players evading a tackle.

They laughed as they ran, the air growing more frigid with each near miss. But in the darkness of the stadium it was impossible to see them all, and he got blasted twenty feet from freedom. She burst into a triumphant laugh, the sound cut off as she took one in the side.

Sputtering, they dodged the last sprinklers and made it to safety, where they both shivered and laughed. Their clothes, the treats, even the blankets, all were soaked. Now freezing, they left wet footprints as they made their way back to the car.

"Do you lose points for the sprinklers?" he asked, his teeth chattering. "Or gain points?"

"Lose points for the lack of planning," she said, her voice distorted by her shivering, "but I think I gain points for spontaneity."

"I'll concede that," he said.

The car came to life and they huddled in it until the engine warmed enough to blast heat through the vents. Only when they were warm did she turn on the lights and pull out of the lot. He cast a look back and grinned.

"You know, I'll never be able to go to a game without thinking of this night."

"Mission accomplished," she said.

"You know, you've thrown down a gauntlet," he said. "But I'm not going to take it easy on you."

"Oh?" she asked, raising an eyebrow. "What do you intend?"

"To win," he said.

"And what will be your prize?"

You.

He opened his mouth to say the word, but it lodged in his throat. *What's wrong with me?* he thought. After hundreds of dates where he'd always managed to keep himself in control, here he was, losing it.

He threw her a sideways glance. Her hair was wet as was her clothing, her skin glistening with moisture that had yet to evaporate. Again he felt the surge of attraction and again suppressed it.

"I think this is the part where most guys say they would buy you dinner," he said, forcing a laugh to hide his consternation.

For the first time he considered that accepting this challenge could be dangerous. His attraction was evident, and if he had to guess, she was attracted to him as well. Could they go on such dates and keep those emotions in check?

But he couldn't back out now. If he did, it would be tantamount to conceding defeat. No, he was committed. But he would have to be *very* cautious or risk their relationship proceeding farther than he wanted.

"One thing," he asked. "If we're really going to do this challenge of yours, you need to understand—"

"I know," she cut in. "We aren't dating exclusively. I expect you'll continue to ask other girls out, and if someone asks me on a date, I'll likely accept."

She smiled, but the expression was at odds with the hint of irritation in her voice. He would have liked to go into detail, but felt a rare sense of trepidation. If she had asked him to date exclusively, he would have said no, and he didn't want their time to end so quickly, not when it showed such promise.

For a brief moment he considered admitting how much he liked her. He'd dated girls he was attracted to in the past, but the fun of dating always superseded the spark of desire. He'd never said anything because it wouldn't have mattered. Now he found himself uncertain.

"Back to your car?" she asked.

He shook his head. "It doesn't have heat. I'll have Jackson help me pick it up tomorrow."

Evidently in an effort to steer the conversation back to lighter topics, Kate asked about his roommate, and the conversation shifted to Jackson. The city passed in blur as they worked their way back to his house, where she parked and laughed nervously.

"I've never walked a guy to his door before."

"I've never been walked to my door before."

"Protocol?" she asked.

"I find a hug is usually best," he replied.

She got out of the car and came around to open his door. He shivered as the cold air cut into his wet clothes, and they walked briskly to the door. When they reached it he turned and stepped into the embrace. The contact was warm and comfortable. She too seemed to feel it and her arms tightened around his back. Although he wanted to pull away, he lingered for an extra moment.

"Is it weird if I say you're warm?" he asked.

She laughed into his shoulder. "Strangely, not the weirdest compliment I've received."

"Which would be?"

"Your elbows are very pointy."

He grimaced. "That's terrible. A guy actually said that to you?"

"In the seventh grade," she said.

"Are they?"

"Of course not." She stepped back and showed him her elbow. "See for yourself."

72

"They're nice elbows," he said with a grin. "Any more bad compliments?"

"Loads, unfortunately."

"Then it appears we have our game for next time," he said. "Tales of our worst dates."

"Now I know I'll win," she said.

She began to shiver again, and he frowned. He wanted to spend more time with her, but it was late, and he'd never asked a girl to stay after a date. She smiled knowingly and took a step towards her car.

"I had a nice time," he said.

She grinned and lowered her voice. "I'll call you."

"Will you really?" he asked, attempting a girl's voice.

"Nope," she said, laughing as she retreated to the warmth of her car. "I'll shoot you a vague text in a few days that has you wondering about my intentions."

He snorted a laugh. Then she shut the door and a moment later the car pulled out of the driveway. Although he was freezing, he remained on the porch until she drove away, wondering if he was in over his head.

Chapter 13

When Kate's car was gone Reed stepped to his door and unlocked it. He swung it open and found Jackson and Shelby rising from the couch where they'd been watching a movie. Both bore expressions of intense curiosity.

"How'd it go?" they asked in unison.

"You expect me to dish on the details?" Reed asked.

"You said you would," Shelby said. "And why are you wet?"

"Nothing happened," Reed said. "But she said she'd call."

While his girlfriend laughed, Jackson scowled. "Don't give me that. You're date like a machine, and when you finally meet your match all you can say is she'll call?"

Reed divested himself of his wet jacket and hung it on the hook. "She issued a challenge."

"What sort of challenge?" Shelby asked.

"We trade off planning dates and see if we can top each other," he said.

"A *dating* challenge?" his roommate asked, his voice rising in disbelief.

A slow smile spread on Jackson's face, prompting Shelby to crow in delight. "She must like you," she said.

"It sounds fun," Reed said evasively.

"Liar," Shelby pounced. "You *do* like her."

"We got drenched in the sprinklers at the stadium," he said. "I'm going to take a shower."

"You can't evade the question forever," Jackson said.

"Yes I can," he called as he left the living room behind.

He heard them fall to speculation as he grabbed a towel and went into the bathroom. He turned on the hot water and stripped before stepping into the shower. After the freezing water and the night air, the hot water was blissful, and for several moments he simply relished the heat. Then his thoughts turned to Kate.

As he considered the challenge and its ramifications he settled on two conclusions. First, the next few months were going to be tremendous fun. And second, dating Kate was dangerous, for his rules and for him.

He stayed in the shower until the water began to cool, an unfortunately brief period in their aged house. Then he stepped out and wrapped a towel around his body. Wiping the moisture off the mirror, he stared at his reflection.

"Are you sure you want to do this?" he asked aloud.

He grinned, realizing the better question would be, *how much do I really like this girl?* As he stared at his reflection a wry smile spread on his face, the answer coming as quickly as the question.

Too much.

His smile widened. "Let the challenge begin."

Part 3: The St. Patrick's Date

Chapter 14

"I expected Reed to call." Ember complained.

Kate sighed. "It's only been a week, and the challenge is for every two weeks."

"He still should have called," Ember said tersely.

Kate sat with her roommates at the kitchen table. Brittney had cooked her famous Bold Chili Enchiladas, a tradition for Thursdays, and only Marta was absent. Their fourth roommate would be home any minute from work. No one missed Brittney's cooking.

"I agree with Ember," Brittney said, poking her head into the kitchen doorway. "He should have called."

"We aren't dating exclusively," Kate said in exasperation. "He doesn't have to call me every day."

Ember folded her arms. "Not dating exclusively is just code for the guy to—,"

"Ember," Kate said sharply. "We both know he's not like that."

"He's still a guy," Brittney said from behind the stove. "And two dates is not enough to know a guy."

Kate looked away, annoyed that she'd begun to agree with her roommates. She'd told Reed they were not exclusive, but she'd *hoped* he would call. Or was she expecting too much from him? Was he just like her roommates said?

She liked him more than she'd told her roommates and secretly hoped the dating challenge would lead to a relationship. At least that's what she thought. Not calling for a week after their second date did not bode well—even if they were not exclusive.

The door burst open and Marta rushed in. "Did he call?"

"No," Ember said, drawing out the syllable to insert a world of disdain.

Marta hung her purse and joined them at the table. "He should have called."

Kate grunted sourly. "Do we even know what to expect? Reed isn't like a normal guy."

"True," Marta said. "But he hasn't even talked to me in class."

Kate's eyes narrowed. "I used his roommate against him," she said. "Any chance *you* have turned against *me*?"

There was a chorus of protests, but Kate leaned back and folded her arms, skewering each of them with a look. Her roommates were her closest friends, but she knew they would lie in an instant if they thought it would be for her benefit.

"Honestly," Brittney said, standing in the doorway to the kitchen with her hands on her hips. "How can you not trust us?"

Kate leveled a finger at her. "You set me up on a Valentine's Day blind date," she said, "and didn't tell me until half an hour before he arrived so I couldn't escape."

"It worked, didn't it?" Ember said airily.

"Exactly," Kate pounced. "You would bribe the dean if you thought it would make me happy."

"Perhaps not the dean," Marta said. "But certainly a professor."

"So you *do* know something," Kate said, leaning in.

Ember shook her head. "We honestly don't. I'd be the first to join a plan against you, but he hasn't given me the opportunity."

The disappointment on her face was too real to be feigned. Ember *wanted* to be involved, to plot Kate's romance to the utmost detail, but Reed had not included her. Ember's irritation at being equally in the dark was comforting, and Kate leaned back in her chair.

"Would you tell me if he tried to use you?" she asked.

"Of course!" Marta exclaimed.

"No," Ember said with a smug smile.

"Whose side are you on?" Brittney asked.

"Kate's love life," Ember said emphatically, causing them all to laugh.

"How close is dinner?" Marta asked. "I had to skip lunch so I'm starving."

"You can't rush perfection," Brittney said with a pointed look at Kate. Then she smiled. "But it's ready now."

She disappeared and a moment later returned with a steaming pan. She placed it on the pad at the center of the table amidst a round of praise, and then served them all. Kate dug in and savored the combination of flavors unique to Brittney's cooking.

"Honestly, Brit," Ember said, "if you cooked like this for a guy, he'd never leave."

"I don't want him to love my cooking," she replied. "I want him to love my body."

She slapped her stomach and laughed. Although it was said in amusement, there was a touch of regret to her words, and Kate exchanged a look with Ember. Brittney never complained about her weight, but she took a noticeably smaller portion of the dinner, suggesting she was trying to lose weight again.

As they ate and talked, Kate's thoughts remained on Reed. Why hadn't he called? For the first time she considered the possibility that he wasn't really attracted to her, and it was still just a game to him.

After she'd issued her dating challenge, she'd half-expected him to call the next day. She knew him well enough to know he hadn't forgotten, and a part of her imagined him agonizing over what to do on their next date. But she didn't like the waiting, and it rankled to feel like he'd forgotten.

As they were finishing dinner the doorbell rang. Sitting closest to the door, Marta took a final bite and stood. "I'll get it!" she said, the exclamation muffled by the food in her mouth.

"Don't talk with your mouth full," Brittney said, and then took a bite and added. "Unless you can do it without anyone noticing."

Kate joined in the laughter but glanced to the door, hoping and wondering if it would be Reed. Marta opened the door but the door blocked the view. She didn't speak, and instead she stepped back into the room and looked to Kate.

"I think it's for you," she said.

"Who is it?" Kate asked.

Marta's expression lit with delight. "Let's just say he doesn't need to call anymore."

It took a moment for her words to sink in and then all three scrambled to the door. Positioned the furthest away, Kate arrived last, a fact for which she complained loudly as she pushed her way through her roommates. Then she spotted what was on the porch and came to a halt, all complaints forgotten.

A black kettle sat on the porch. The reflective material that lined the interior of the kettle enhancing the light placed in the center so it looked like it contained gold. But instead of coins it was filled with skittles. Pounds and pounds of skittles.

Ember stepped outside and scanned the street like a hawk hunting prey, but there was no sign of Reed or his car. Kate did a cursory look but did not expect to find him, and instead picked up the surprisingly heavy kettle and brought it into the living room.

"I don't understand," Marta said as they all knelt around the kettle. "What does a pot of skittles have to do with anything?"

Kate's eyes flew to the calendar on the wall, to the date the following week. "St. Patrick's day," she exclaimed. "It's next Saturday."

Brittney picked up a handful of skittles and let them sprinkle through her hand. "And he sent you the end of the rainbow," she said.

Her heart beating in her chest, Kate realized she'd made a fatal flaw. She'd assumed Reed would ask her on a date the normal way—but his creative dating was anything but normal. And she'd issued a challenge, one he'd said he intended to win.

"There's a note," Ember said, and grabbed the piece of paper sticking out of the skittles. Kate snatched it from her hands and read it first, the other girls crowding to read over her shoulder.

You are invited to attend the _____

At the _____ *at* _____

Attire should be expendable.

"What's with the blanks?" Kate asked.

"Maybe he wants you to figure it out," Ember said, turning the paper over to examine the back.

Kate frowned in confusion, and then her eyes fell on the skittles. One was different than the others. Instead of an S, it had a different letter—a W. She reached in and picked it up, and found that a marker had been used to change the lettering.

"The answer is in here," Kate said, pointing to the pot of skittles. "And we have to find it."

Marta paused with a handful of skittles halfway to her mouth. "So I shouldn't eat them?"

"Not until we find the ones with the letters," Ember said sternly, and took charge like a diminutive general. "Get the cookie sheets. We're going to need some space."

Excited at the strange invitation, Kate dived into the task. Her roommates complained that there were so many skittles but with each found letter there were cries of delight, and it didn't take long to find them all. Then they began sorting them in an attempt to decipher what they meant.

"10:00," Brittney said. "There's no other time it could be." She placed the numbers on the note.

It took several more minutes before they figured out the letters, but when they did Kate was even more confused. Ember grabbed a pen and filled them in on the paper. Then they all sat back and stared at the text.

"It's at President's Park," Ember said. "Saturday morning."

Kate shook her head in confusion. "But what's a Color War?"

Chapter 15

Kate pulled into the crowded parking lot and claimed one the few empty spots. Before leaving the car she checked herself in the mirror. She knew it was foolish to be nervous, but the prospect of another date with Reed made her heart thump in her chest.

Dressed in torn jeans and a faded shirt, her clothes were certainly expendable. Ember had insisted she wear nicer clothing, but Kate had argued that doing so would make her more uncomfortable than dressing down.

"Besides," Kate had said. "It won't take long before my clothing will be covered in paint."

It had taken them all of five minutes to find the answer to Reed's invitation. Set in President's Park in downtown Boulder, the Color War was a battle of the rainbow each St. Patrick's Day. Similar to a color run, participants used balloons filled with tinted foam to wage war against each other. The pictures had shown hundreds of adults and youth plastered in every color, their clothing unrecognizable beneath the paint. All three of Kate's roommates had wanted to participate, but Kate had insisted.

"It's not appropriate to bring your roommates on a date."

She exited the car and joined the throng of people working their way into the depths of the park. Many carried plastic shields, others wore paintball masks, and some came with large water guns. Festive and exciting, the atmosphere brought a nervous smile to her face as she pushed her way through the crowd. Her fears at not finding Reed didn't last, and she spotted him standing at the edge of the lot.

"I see you got my message," he said with a smile.

"It took an hour to find all the letters," she said, raising her voice to be heard over the excited crowd.

He laughed. "My favorite dates are those that begin with a creative invitation."

She noticed the allusion to herself and laughed nervously, but he was already guiding her into the crowd. As they approached the center of the park it became clear that many participants already knew where to go, with teams forming of the various colors.

"What color are we?" she asked.

"Blue," he replied. "It's your favorite, isn't it?"

She scowled. "My roommates said you didn't enlist them."

"They didn't," he said, and his easy smile returned. "Girls usually wear their favorite color on a first date, and so I guessed."

Pleased that he'd remembered such a detail, she gestured vaguely in the direction of her house. "You really didn't use my roommates?"

"Not this time," he replied, his blue eyes sparkling with humor.

"So roommates are fair game?" she asked.

"For both sides," he said.

She caught the double meaning. She could manipulate Reed's roommate, but Reed was just as able to turn him back to his own side. Like pawns in their challenge, the roommates would be enlisted and coerced at every turn.

They reached their army's location and found dozens of individuals dressed in blue. Arming themselves with water guns and balloons, they were preparing for war. The air gained the edge of anticipation as they armed themselves, and someone offered Kate a bandoleer of water balloons. She laughed and draped it around her neck like a sash at a beauty contest.

"How do I look?" she asked, affecting a model pose.

"Flawless," he said, and collected a water gun from a stack.

Several large barrels were scattered about the area and most players were busy filling their weapons. Some just filled buckets, laughing like they were imagining dumping it on someone's head. Caught up in the rising tension, Kate picked up a smaller gun and gave it an experimental squirt, accidently striking Reed in the chest.

He laughed. "You're supposed to try and hit the *other* colors."

"Sorry!" she exclaimed.

A nearby woman giggled and sprayed her husband. "That's okay, dear," she said. "Hit him when his back is turned."

The husband laughed and sprayed her back, painting her side a bright blue. Others converged on the spot and Kate realized that the paint was a catalyst, inviting everyone to join in the fight. She hastily retreated, but a booming voice saved her from dying an azure death.

"Happy St. Patrick's Day!" an amplified voice shouted, drawing all eyes to the clearing between the armies. Dressed in garish green, a leprechaun waved his hands and welcomed them all to the color war. As his welcome speech came to a close, he checked his watch. "You have sixty seconds to ready yourselves. The war ends when you are out of ammunition. Good luck!"

Kate laughed, unable to contain her nervous excitement. "What now?"

Reed met her gaze, his eyes filled with a wild delight. "We fight."

He caught her hand and her rapidly beating heart increased its flutter, but he was merely guiding her to a section of trees overlooking the clearing. Then he leaned against the tree like a soldier.

"Oh," he said, reaching into a pocket, "you'll want these."

He tossed her a pair of glasses, obviously intended to prevent paint in the eye, and then donned a pair of his own. She fumbled with the glasses as the speaker began to count down from thirty, the other colors joining in the chant.

At ten seconds clouds of colored smoke erupted in the clearing and surrounding trees, the smoke quickly obscuring trees and leaves, paths and benches. Kate swallowed as she leaned against a tree and looked to Reed.

"Are you ready?" he asked.

"No!" she shouted.

"Too late!" He laughed as the great *boom* signaled the start of the war.

With a deafening shout the five armies rushed the clearing and began firing indiscriminately. Balloons were hurled into the fray and colored water blasted the erstwhile warriors. Laughter and shouts of dismay filled the clouded scene as smoke drifted across the battlefield.

"Watch the right!" Reed shouted.

She swiveled and found a group of purples ascending the slope, attempting to flank the blues. They saw each other and both began to fire. But Kate was behind the tree, so the paint splashed against the trunk, scattering color across her side as she unloaded on them.

Reed joined her on the other side of the oak tree and fired with her, but there were too many, and some came at their side. Purple splashed across her hip, causing her to laugh in surprise. She grabbed a water balloon from the sash and hurled it at them, and then another. The foes turned out to be two young men, both of whom scampered away under the sudden assault.

Caught up in the moment, she turned back to those charging up the slope and fired, striking each with precision. Her accuracy drew a shout from Reed, who fired at her side, protecting her flank.

"Where did you learn to aim?" he called.

"Military family," she said. "Remember?" Then she spotted a group of yellow coming from the opposite side. "Look out!"

Caught between orange and purple, they were pummeled with color, and in seconds, water and foam stained them from head to toe. With adrenaline in her veins Kate ran and twisted, dodging tree trunks and other colors as she sought to escape. Reed stayed with her every step, and together they fought the horde of color.

Through the haze of smoke, they ran straight into an all-out brawl, with paint, foam, and smoke filling the air. The crowd had dissolved into a confusing war, casting paint at each other, heedless of the original armies. Kate sprayed a woman twice before recognizing her as the one who'd targeted her husband before the war. Her apology was met with a spray of blue and a giggle.

In the haze of color and smoke, Kate looked at Reed. His features were obscured by layers of paint, but his eyes shone the brightest. Even through the glasses speckled with green, they pierced into her, an unspoken challenge, an invitation to stand at his side. She smiled and stood at his back, and in the midst of a war she marveled at the sense of home.

Chapter 16

The color war seemed to last for hours, but barely topped twenty minutes before everyone was out of ammunition. Plastered with every color of the rainbow, the disparate armies now stood together, and none could distinguish who had come from where. Shouting and laughter filled the park and there was much smearing of paint as people tried to wipe their faces clean.

Trees looked like a color bomb had exploded in their branches, the colors reaching surprisingly high and staining the leaves. The ground was a tapestry of vivid colors and footprints, interspersed by patches of mud.

Reed's black hair had turned a bright green, but a patch over his ear was all orange. Purple dripped down his face onto his shoulder. Splotches of red trickled down his glasses and onto his chin, darkening the yellow on his chest.

"You've never looked better," Kate said with a laugh.

She reached up and attempted to wipe the paint off his face, succeeding only in smearing the colors together. He protested and did the same to her, causing her to fend him off before he could make the mess worse. Paint splattered nearby people, nearly causing a renewed conflict.

Reed wiped the paint from his hands. "I've always wanted to do this war."

She looked up from wiping color from her arms. "I assumed you'd done this before," she said.

"Nope," he said. "I heard about it a couple years ago but never had a date I thought would appreciate it."

"So why me?" she asked.

"You'd mentioned your family had been military," he said. "I hoped it had rubbed off on you. You're certainly a good shot." He pointed to her water gun leaning against her leg.

"I used to go shooting with my brothers and my dad," she said. "My brothers would complain that I was better, but I think they let me win."

He raised a purple eyebrow. "You'll have to teach me to shoot."

"You certainly need it," she said with a laugh. "You missed more than my grandmother."

"Hey!" he protested. "I contributed."

"To our loss," she said.

He laughed. "I can't tell if *anyone* won," he said, gesturing to the paint covered people.

"True," she agreed. Her phone buzzed and she wiped her hand enough to pull it out. She snorted and lifted it up so they could take a picture. "The blondes want to see us post-war."

"It's rapidly becoming a tradition," he said, leaning down so she could snap the picture. He smiled, and then asked, "How's the picture?"

"Colorful," she said.

He grinned. "That's an understatement."

"I don't think I want to get into my car," she said, examining the picture and then herself. "This may wash out, but I can't exactly put my car though the washing machine."

He looked at his own drenched clothing. "In my car the colors would be an upgrade."

She laughed. "Seriously. How are we going to get clean enough to leave?"

Overhearing her question, a nearby girl pointed to the edge of the parking lot. "Don't worry about getting clean. That's the best part."

"What's the best part?" she asked.

"I didn't get the chance to tell you," Reed said. "The fire department should be here any moment."

"The fire department?" she asked, turning to the parking lot.

A fire truck pulled into the lot and flicked its siren, the sound drawing the paint-spattered crowd. The firemen unloaded and began hooking up the hose to the fire hydrant. Realizing their intent, Kate's eyes widened.

"Don't tell me they're going to . . ."

"Yep," Reed grinned.

"No," she breathed.

The firemen opened the top and water exploded from the hose. Aimed upward so as not to knock anyone down, the geyser became a sudden rainstorm that washed the colors from their bodies.

Kate gasped as freezing water fell on her and she wrapped her arms tightly around her chest. Shivering, she tried to escape, but the press of bodies did not allow it. Then Reed shook his hair, sending paint and water onto her.

"This is not how I like to shower!" she exclaimed.

He merely laughed and wiped his face clean. All around them others were doing the same, rinsing the colors into the ground at their feet. Many stood huddled against the cold, while the more adventurous danced about, calling for more.

Eager to escape the chill, Kate rinsed what she could. By the time the hose was shut off she was drenched, but passably clean. Her feet squished in the mud as they exited the park and made their way to Reed's car.

"I have towels," he said.

"Of course you do," she said, shivering.

March had warmed considerably from February, but it had yet to fully embrace spring. Everyone in the lot was busy wrapping towels around their shoulders and drying off, and she noticed several families standing together, the children disappointed that the event was over.

She watched two young girls giggle as they threw lingering paint at each other. Their mother became exasperated in her attempt to usher them into the van. Kate found herself wondering what type of mother she would be.

"Ready?" Reed asked, handing her a towel.

She wrapped it around her shoulders and dried herself off, grateful she hadn't worn clothing that would be revealing when wet. More towels were in the car and she did her best to keep any color from getting on the seat. Reed was less concerned.

"It'll wipe out," he said, turning the car on.

"I've never done anything like this," she said, gesturing to the park.

"There's a lot of fun things to do if you have the inclination to look," Reed said.

"Few have the inclination to look."

He raised an eyebrow at her tone, and she smiled sadly. "I've had several boyfriends," she said. "None would have thought to do this for a date."

"And Jason?"

His question had no animosity, and instead sounded like a concerned friend. She smiled, realizing she'd hardly thought of him since their first date together. Guys didn't want to talk about past relationships, but with Reed that rule seemed not to apply.

"Our most exciting date was to the IHOP," she said with a smile.

"The IHOP can be very exciting," he agreed. "But only when you order from their secret menu."

"They have a secret menu?"

"Of course," he said. "Their bacon and banana stack is divine."

She looked out the window and watched the van she'd seen earlier. The parents were done buckling their children and stood outside their door. Their words were not audible but their kiss said it all. She was surprised she hadn't noticed the father before, but now that she looked around, she noticed a handful of fathers also with their children.

She cast a surreptitious glance at Reed. His attention was on the traffic attempting to leave the lot, and he didn't notice her scrutiny. A few patches of paint were still on his face and lightening his black hair, but the color only seemed to make him more attractive.

She found herself wondering if her dating challenge would work. Would he fall for her? Or was she just a game? Abruptly he glanced her way. Caught, she grinned and pointed to the van, where the father was just climbing into the driver's seat.

"It's good to see a father playing with his kids," she said.

"I wouldn't know," he said. "That certainly wasn't mine."

"Do you think they start out good? Or do they become good fathers after they're married?"

"Are you asking how to know if a guy will be a good father?"

"I suppose I am," she said.

He laughed lightly. "You mentioned marriage last time, and now fatherhood. Do you always talk about such heavy topics on dates?"

She shrugged. "I'm curious. You've been on what, hundreds of dates? Surely you have an idea of what the girl would be like in the future."

He scratched at a piece of paint on his check. "Some of those I've dated are now married, and I've seen them with their husbands."

"Really?"

"My roommate met his girlfriend because she went on a date with me."

Kate snorted in amusement. "And that's not awkward?"

"It would have been," he said, and threw her a smile, "if I hadn't held to my rules."

For the first time Kate considered his dating rules beyond the context of a single date. With no intimacy there was little risk of drama, and friends could stay friends. She frowned as she recalled a former friend.

"Sandy Wilson," she said aloud.

"Who?"

"We were friends our junior year in high school," Kate said. "We both liked the same guy but he became my boyfriend. Then I found out they were sleeping together, and never talked to her again."

"Sounds like it was hard," he replied.

"It was," she said. "I really liked him. He was the one I lost my . . ."

She'd never had qualms about admitting the depth of her past relationships before, but with Reed she found herself flushing in embarrassment. Reed clearly understood but he shifted the topic with ease, saving her from finishing the sentence.

"Ready for lunch?"

"Does it involve paint?" she asked warily.

He smiled. "Not this time."

Chapter 17

As they drove through town they talked about the color war like two players reminiscing about a great game. Reed had seen a guy take a water balloon in the face, while Kate had spotted a kid wearing combat fatigues running around screaming with his father. Similarly garbed, the man tried to keep his son under control.

They laughed and talked all the way to another park, this one all but hidden at the corner of the city. Reed pulled into the empty lot and he found a spot. Sufficiently dry, Kate exited the vehicle to examine the out-of-the way spot.

Overgrown shrubs and trees dotted the park, while the lack of cars indicated it was rarely used. Containing a small playground and a basketball court, the park offered little else except a few stretches of grass. Forest surrounded the park like a baseball glove around a ball.

A sign indicated the park would soon be replaced with a subdivision, and Kate suspected that few had lamented its loss. Still, the grass was cut and the court was clean, and she liked the solitude after the color war.

"What are we doing here?" she asked.

"Lunch," he responded. "I hope you're good at basketball."

She turned to find him closing his trunk, a bag of basketballs in his hand. Each had been covered in a different color, turning them into a rainbow. He grinned as he pointed to the basketball court in the park.

"It's St. Patrick's Day," he said. "And what would it be without a rainbow and a pot of gold?"

Now that he'd pointed it out, she spotted the wrapping around the hoop. Black paper had been taped around the rim and net to resemble a large cauldron. She grinned and walked with him towards the court.

"Does anyone ever think your dates are stupid?"

"Of course not." Then his lips twitched and he amended. "Sometimes."

She laughed. "Where's lunch?"

"We have to earn it," he replied. "Once we've each scored the rainbow, we get to eat."

"What if I finish before you?"

He grinned. "Then you get to enjoy the show while you eat."

"Challenge accepted."

They reached the court and Kate spotted the chalk lines placed on the court. Red was closest to the hoop, while purple was a half-court shot, the rest staggered in their distance and angle. He placed the balls at their appropriate spots and then returned to the red, a layup.

"Ladies first," he said.

She accepted the ball and banked it into the 'cauldron' with ease. He made the same attempt, but it ricocheted off with a *clang*, and she erupted in laughter. He flashed a mock scowl and stabbed a finger to orange at the free-throw line.

"I'll catch up."

"Sure you will," she said.

He laughed, and for the next several minutes they traded shots. It quickly became evident that he was decent, but lacked the skill of a seasoned player. She'd played with her brothers and father, and learned to shoot from them. Within fifteen minutes she finished blue, a three-point shot from the corner.

"It appears I underestimated you," he said, still standing at yellow.

"Do you always pick activities you can't win?" she asked innocently.

He flashed his easy smile. "Perhaps."

95

She paused in dribbling the ball as she realized he hadn't chosen basketball because it was *his* talent. He'd done it to discover *hers*. Most guys wanted to demonstrate their superiority. She'd always found it irritating to watch a guy strut like a peacock fanning his tail feathers.

And guys who lost to girls frequently became annoyed. She cast him a sideways look, but saw no hint of irritation. He seemed amused at her skill. After Jason, who loved sports but thought her place was to sit on the sideline, she'd forgotten what it was like to feel supported.

Distracted, her first attempt at the half-court shot missed wide. He collected the ball and tossed it back to her, and then shot his own, which bounced off the rim and out. Laughing at his own miss, he gestured to her.

"This is the wildest game of horse I've ever played," she said.

"I as well," he replied.

"Do you always do themed dates?"

He shrugged. "When the occasion permits. In my experience girls like a theme."

"And guys don't care," she said, lining up another shot, and another miss.

"True," he said, finally making the yellow shot with a lucky bounce.

His celebration ended abruptly as her half court shot swished the net and came out of the cauldron. She laughed at his crestfallen expression and caught the ball when it bounced by. Then she stepped to him.

"I'm famished," she said brightly. "Where's lunch?"

"In the box," he said. "Try not to finish before I do."

"I'll eat slow," she said.

She took a seat next to the box and leaned against a tree. The lunch proved to be entirely green, with even the bread of the sandwiches a shade of the color. As she sipped the green tea she watched him attempting the half-court shot.

"This is delicious," she called.

"I'm glad you're enjoying it!"

He shot.

And missed.

"You did say the meal came with a show," she said.

He laughed as he collected the ball and tried again. "I live to entertain."

"You're doing it wrong," she called out.

He held up the ball. "This may come as a surprise," he said, "but my family is full of nerds."

"You didn't play *any* sports?"

"Chess."

She laughed. "Is that all?"

"I played lacrosse in high school," he said with a smile, "and I do snowboard."

"But not basketball."

"Nope."

She stood and left the lunch behind. Joining him at the half court line, she took the ball from him and showed him how to hold it. Then she tossed it into the air, rolling her hand so it added a nice spin.

"You have to loft the ball," she said, and smiled as she added, "like a rainbow."

He gave a passable attempt as he shot the ball, but again it bounced off the rim. "It might as well be a mile," he said.

She stepped to the bouncing ball and caught it. Returning to him, she said, "You need to aim for the back of the hoop, not the front."

He shot again. "How much did you play?"

"Every week," she said, smiling at the memory. "Baker, my oldest brother, would always play on my team and I would guard my dad."

"Did they take it easy on you?"

"When I was a kid," she said. "But when I started making three's my dad started guarding me."

"I never really got the chance to play basketball," he said. "My sister wasn't interested in sports and my mom was too busy working to take me to games after my dad left."

"That's too bad," she said. "You have promise, but you're holding the ball wrong."

She picked up the ball from the latest miss and handed it to Reed. Then she reached up and stabilized his hands on the ball, moved his other hand to the side. She shifted his fingers, the act forcing her to lean against him.

All at once she became conscious of the contact, of her hand pressed against his, the feel of his skin. She swallowed, the soft touch sparking heat down her arm and into her stomach. Her eyes flicked to him and found his gaze on her. She could feel every curve of his hip against hers.

"Is that how you do it?" he murmured.

"That's how you do it," she said softly.

She retreated and focused on the hoop, directing him to shoot. With her back to him she imagined his hand snaking around her stomach, pulling her close to kiss her neck. The image was so vivid she trembled, but he didn't close the gap.

"Whenever you're ready," she said.

Out of the corner of her eye she saw him bend and shoot, and the ball soared through the air. It bounced off the back of the hoop and sank into the net, re-emerging from the cauldron fastened to the rim. The shot broke the spell of the moment and she nodded in satisfaction.

"You're getting better."

"I'm getting lucky," he said. "Without you I would have been out here all day."

"On that we can agree," she said.

He gestured to the meal in the shade. "Ready to eat?"

"I was ready before you," she said. "Remember?"

He laughed. "I suspect you won't let me forget."

"Never," she said, but her eyes dropped to his hands, which he held at his side. It may have been her imagination, but it seemed there was a rigidity to his arms, as if he were holding himself in check.

Chapter 18

They ate in the shade, and although he noticed several piercing looks, neither commented on the moment on the court. As she added green croutons to her salad the conversation turned from the date to the past.

"Have you ever had a serious girlfriend?" she asked.

"Will you judge me if I say no?"

"No," she said with a smile. "Have you ever had a girlfriend at all?"

"Three," he replied. "Two in high school and one in elementary school. But that lasted a few hours, so I'm not sure it counts."

"It doesn't," she said with a smile.

"Two then," he said. "You?"

"Four," she said. "Three before Jason, none of which lasted long."

"Which was the one that honked from the street?" he asked, his lips twitching in amusement.

"That would be number two," she said. "My brothers called him Gassy because he would only buy premium gas for his car."

"Sounds like a real winner," he said.

"Disney teaches that frogs turn into princes," she said. "But in my experience most are just frogs."

"Did your brothers nickname all your boyfriends?"

"All," she said with a sigh. "Even the non-boyfriends."

"What was Jason's nickname?"

She hesitated. "Nappy."

"Why?"

"They said he was so bland they fell asleep when I talked about him."

Reed laughed. "Your brothers sound delightful."

"They're your typical overprotective military brothers," she said.

"I would have liked to have a brother," Reed said, sipping his drink. "I suppose when my sister gets married I'll have one, but you never know who a sibling is going to end up with."

"True," she said. "My oldest brother has a serious girlfriend and she's . . . a bit much."

"In what way?"

"Let's just say she puts makeup on to go to the gym."

He laughed. "There's nothing wrong with girls like that. I wouldn't take them on a date like this, though." He swept his hand at the court.

"What would you do?"

"Take them to a spa."

"Really?" she asked.

He grinned. "I took a girl to a seaweed wrap, and she was so happy to have a guy willing to go to spas that she thought I loved her. I didn't, and it didn't end well."

"You know, we never got to talk about our worst dates," she said. "That was a game I could win."

"It was your idea," he said, pointing his fork at her. "I assumed you'd want to run that game."

"Our next date, then," she said, with a smile. "And I expect you to come prepared."

"I've had my fair share of dates end poorly," he said. "Not every girl is what I expect, and not every date can be researched."

"I'm surprised you didn't enlist the blondes for this date," she said.

"I considered it," he said. "But I get the impression they'll turn on me in a heartbeat."

"They are nothing if not loyal," she agreed with a smile.

He smiled in turn, his blue eyes sparkling with mischief. "I do have a few ideas that just might persuade them to my side."

She laughed. "As we agreed, roommates and friends are fair game."

"So what were the other boyfriend's nicknames?" he asked.

"Screech and Pirate."

"There has to be a story behind those names," he said, adding ranch to his salad.

"Screech was skinny and tall," she said with a sigh. "But his voice hadn't matured yet, so his voice would crack whenever he got nervous."

"And your brother probably made him nervous," he said.

"By intention," she agreed.

"It's a brother's duty to protect his sister from boys that don't measure up," he said.

"So you did the same?" she asked.

He pulled out a smaller pot from the box, but this one was full of chocolate gold coins. Smiling, he put the pot between them and unwrapped one for himself. She did the same, and as she savored the chocolate he nodded.

"I preferred more covert methods of protecting my sister."

She snorted a laugh, nearly sending chocolate up her nose. "I bet you did!"

"What about Pirate?" he asked, steering the conversation back to her.

"He really liked Johnny Depp."

"The actor?"

She nodded. "Really, *really* liked him. He had posters, stickers, and collectable action figures from the Pirates of Caribbean movies."

"Isn't that a little juvenile?" he asked.

"We were thirteen," she admitted. "We were all juvenile."

He smiled wryly. "It's times like these I'm glad I was in the friend zone. It allowed me to hide my awkwardness."

"And what awkwardness was that?" she asked, biting her chocolate and blinking her eyes innocently.

His eyes narrowed. "Oh no," he said, "I'm not going to tell that easily."

"Why not?" she coaxed. "It's not like anyone is going to overhear."

She scooted a bit closer and leaned in like he would share a secret. Reed shook his head, but she remained in place, her expression expectant. Finally he shook his head and pointed his chocolate at her.

"Those eyes cannot be refused, you know that? They're like the brightest emeralds."

He'd said it in jest, but she heard Jason's voice. She looked away, her smile evaporating. Noticing the sudden change in her demeanor, he sat silent for a moment. Then he grunted under his breath.

"Jason?"

She turned back, her eyebrows pulling together. "How did you know?"

"Dating is a minefield," he said. "That particular expression was one of regret. Did he say that about you?"

Disconcerted by his perceptiveness, she nodded. "He always said my eyes were like liquid emeralds."

"On that we can agree," he said with a faint smile. "Although it's not your best feature."

"What would that be?" she asked, stung. She'd always thought of her eyes as her most striking asset.

"Isn't it obvious?" he asked, taking a bite. "Your courage."

She sat back. "What do you mean?"

He held her gaze for a moment, his blue eyes piercing into her as if they could read her soul. "I've been on a thousand dates," he said, "and not once has a girl asked me out like you have."

She laughed to cover her flush. "I don't feel courageous."

"A recent acquisition?" he asked, raising an eyebrow. Then he shook his head. "Or perhaps Jason never saw it."

She considered his words, her mind drawn back to their relationship. Jason had always been leading, always stepping in front, always wanting to teach her, to be in charge. She'd fallen into the role of follower but looking back she realized she'd never quite been content. A part of her had resented her place, and when he'd proposed that part had balked.

"Do you always read your dates so effectively?" she asked.

"Usually," he admitted. "But only by necessity. If I couldn't tell what a girl liked, the dates would fall flat—which they have, on occasion."

"Really?"

His lips twitched. "I'll save the stories for your game on worst dates."

She helped clean up the lunch and retrieved some of the basketballs. He grabbed a stool placed behind the pole and reached up to disconnect the hoop cauldron. Then they loaded everything into the box and walked to the car.

"Anything else?" she asked.

"Was it not enough?" he asked.

She smiled. "It was plenty. I'll be hard pressed to top it."

"I figured you and the blonds had already planned your next strike," he said, his voice muffled as he loaded the box into the car.

"Nope," she said. "We were distracted."

"With classes?"

"No," she said. "Because a certain guy didn't call."

"Who didn't . . ." Reed's eyes widened and he began to laugh. "You thought I would call to ask you out."

"I did," she admitted. "But then, I've never heard of a creative way to ask a girl out."

"Let's call it an . . . advanced technique," he said with a smile.

She folded her arms and leaned against the car. "You realize that most guys these days ask a girl out via text."

"That's not very respectful," he said, unlocking her door and opening it for her. "Or do you like being asked out by a text?"

"No," she said. "It's almost as bad as breaking up over text."

He shut the door and walked around, but his door jammed. He bumped it with his hip and then pulled it open. A moment later they were leaving the park behind. As they pulled back onto the main road he gestured to her.

"The way a guy asks a girl reflects how he will treat her on the date."

"You sound like my grandfather," she said.

"I learned it from my grandfather," he said with a smile. "Doesn't mean it's not true."

"So now I have to ask you in a creative way?"

"Of course not," he said, and threw her a sly smile. "You can always concede defeat."

"Never," she said.

"Good," he said. "I wouldn't want to win this competition too early."

She stole a glance. His comment was said to tease but she thought she noticed a trace of desire to his tone. She hoped it meant he wanted the competition for more than just the game. Or was that all she was?

Chapter 19

They left the hidden park behind and he drove her to her car, but at her request, he turned towards her house instead. She'd noticed there was still dried paint on her clothes and did not want to transfer any to her car.

"I'd rather clean up," she said. "One of my roommates will help me get my car."

He obliged, and drove her home. When they reached the driveway he exited and opened the door for her. She stood and spotted three faces plastered against the window pane and jerked her hand, signaling them away. Reed smiled as he noticed the motion.

"They want to know about your date."

"They wanted to come to the color war," she said.

"Really?"

She nodded. "I didn't think it was appropriate to bring my roommates onto the date. Ember would grill you like a CIA operative."

He laughed. "One of these days we should set up a group date."

As they walked towards the porch she raised an eyebrow. "I got the impression you didn't do group dates."

"I prefer single dates now," he said, "but most of my early attempts were in pairs or larger. It's easier to keep the conversation going."

They reached the porch and she turned to him. He smiled and opened his arms, drawing her into an embrace. They were mostly dry but she could feel his body against her, and smiled at the contact before pulling away.

"I'm lucky to have you as my date," he said.

"See you soon," she replied with a laugh.

He grinned and walked away, but she waited until he'd pulled back onto the street. Then she turned to the door, which swung open before she could turn the handle. She found herself facing all three of the blondes.

"How was the war?" Ember asked.

"Colorful," she said, gesturing to the lingering stains on her clothing.

"You should come in," Marta said in a rush. "I'm sure you want to get cleaned up."

"Don't you want to hear about my date?" she asked.

Brittney shook her head. "After you get cleaned up."

Kate paused in the process of removing her shoes, her eyes drifting between her roommates. She'd expected them to pounce the moment she walked in the door, but now they seemed reluctant to hear about the date. Ember shifted her feet impatiently, making Kate suspicious.

"What's going on?" she asked.

"Just go to your room," Marta said. "Please?"

Confused, Kate walked to her room and swung the door open—and froze in shock. Her room was covered in Saint Patrick's Day decorations. Green candy littered the floor, leprechauns hung from the walls, and shamrocks spun on string.

"Did you do this?" she asked.

"Nope," Ember said, all but bouncing on her feet as she pointed to the card on the bed.

She picked up the card and opened it to reveal a simple note.

I'm lucky to have you as my date.

Until next time.

Reed

"Reed did this?" she asked, turning to her roommates and holding up the card. "When?"

"Just after you left," Ember burst. "He knocked on the door and asked if he could decorate your room."

"What if my room was dirty?" Kate asked.

Marta scoffed. "You know it never is."

"I can't believe you betrayed me," Kate said, but she could not restrain her smile.

"He was so cute," Britney said, clearly relieved that she wasn't mad. "He wanted to leave a note for after the date—before you even started. What kind of guy does that?"

"I can't believe how fast he set it up," Ember said. "He must really like you."

Kate smiled and looked down at the card. In the sea of green she read it again, the very words he'd said on the porch—knowing exactly what she was about to find. It was thoughtful, clever, inventive, and surprising. But she couldn't be sure if it was still the game, or if he felt for her what she felt for him. With the power to ask now in her hands, she knew only one thing for certain.

She was going to find out.

Part 4: The Magic Date

Chapter 20

"You're fidgeting again," Jackson said.

Reed sighed. "Sorry."

He was sitting in the living room, ostensibly doing homework. Jackson and his girlfriend sat at the kitchen table, Shelby helping Jackson with his trig homework. With an effort Reed put the pencil down so he wouldn't keep tapping his book.

"You should call Kate," Shelby said.

"It's not like that," he said.

"But it can be," she said.

"Shelby's right," Jackson said. "This whole week you've been fidgeting like a squirrel on speed."

"That's not true," Reed protested.

Jackson stabbed a finger at him. "Yesterday it took you an hour to eat dinner."

"It wasn't that long."

"It's called fast food for a reason," Jackson said.

Reed began gathering his books. "I need to get to class."

"When will you admit you like her?" Shelby asked.

Reed stuffed books into his bag. "You know my rules."

"Rules change," Shelby said. "Or did you think you'd do this dating game forever."

"I'll see you guys later," Reed said, and walked to the door.

Foregoing the jacket, he stepped outside and strode to his car. He climbed into the seat but for a moment just stared at the wheel. Was Shelby right? Did he like Kate that much? He grimaced as another name came to mind.

Aura.

Burying the memories before they could resurface, he jammed the keys into the ignition and turned. Then he backed out of the driveway and made his way to Main Street. Distracted, he nearly hit the curb, and he forced himself to slow down.

It was Thursday morning and traffic was light. Their house was just a few blocks from campus, close enough to bike or walk on the frequent occasions when his Camry decided to take a day off. The belt squealed as he turned into the parking lot next to the psychology building and turned the car off. Then he reached for his bag, but his hand stopped when he noticed a splash of paint on the seat.

A soft smile spread on his face and he reached out to touch the paint. The color war had been one of his favorite activities, but he couldn't tell what he'd enjoyed more, the day . . . or the date.

He leaned back in his seat with a sigh, wondering if he should end things with Kate before they got more serious. He'd planned their first date like any other, yet never expected such attraction. Her beauty, her intelligence, her subtle courage, all commanded attention.

Leaving his car behind, he trudged to the building and made his way to class. He was early, and only one other student sat in the front row. Taking his usual seat in the middle, Reed pulled out his notebook and pencil and then stared at the map of the brain hanging from the front wall.

The room was large and sloped to the professor's desk at the base. A white board and a projector screen dominated the front wall, while the other walls contained posters of brain hemispheres and chemistry diagrams.

After sixty seconds he noticed the other student glancing his way, a look of irritation on her face. Then he realized he was taping his pencil again, the sound reverberating throughout the silent room.

"Sorry," he said.

The girl grunted and returned her attention to her book. Another classmate came in, and then another. Reed nodded to the one he knew but kept his attention on the white board at the front of the room. He glanced at the clock, but only five minutes had passed.

After going on so many dates he'd grown accustomed to letting go, even if he liked the girl. He'd been attracted to some of the girls he'd taken out, but he'd always been able to stifle that attraction—for all except Kate.

What about her was so vexing? What about her demanded attention? If he could find the answer, perhaps he could suppress the desire. Once he did that, he could enjoy their challenge for what it was, a game.

But was that what he wanted?

He stared at the white board without seeing it, his thoughts on Kate's smile after the color war. Brighter than the colors plastered across her skin, it had conveyed excitement and mischief, a unique sense of adventure.

He imagined ending the dating game, of simply calling Kate and saying he was done. His inability to give an explanation would leave her hurt, but it would be done, and he would never see her again . . .

The very thought caused him to grimace, the prospect of never seeing Kate—let alone hurting her—drawing the scowl to his lips. He'd known the competition would be dangerous, but never considered just how dangerous. Perhaps the question wasn't if he *should* retreat from Kate, but if he *could*.

Other students entered the class and it quickly filled as the hour approached. Then the professor entered and greeted them on her way to her desk. There was still five minutes to class and she liked to review her lesson prior to beginning. Accustomed to her schedule, the other students finished retrieving their books and sending last minute texts before pocketing their phones.

Then another person entered the room. Dressed in a full cloak and pointed hat, he wore nice clothes and an orange and red scarf around his neck. A smattering of laughter drew Reed from his thoughts and he turned to watch the newcomer walk to the front of the classroom.

The resemblance to Harry Potter was uncanny, eliciting titters and stifled laughter. He even had a wand in his hand. Smiling and nodding to the students, he made his way to the front, finally drawing the professor's attention.

"Young man," she asked. "Is there something you need?"

"No, thank you professor," he said in a British accent

He reached the front of the room and withdrew a pole and a black cloth, which he hung on top of the white board. More laughter ensued as the students glanced between the confused professor and the wizard. She rose to her feet, her voice gaining an edge.

"This is *my* classroom," she said. "And you are interrupting."

He glanced at the clock. "Not for three minutes, professor. I'll be done by then." Without waiting for a response, he turned to the class and spoke like they were at a show. "I come to deliver a message, but it is to one, rather than all. I trust the chosen one will understand its meaning." He then pointed his wand at the cloth hanging over the board.

"Wordium Revealium!"

With a stylish flourish he ripped the cloth down from the board, revealing the letters now written there. At no point had he touched the board or put a hand behind the cloth—nevertheless, the text was there in bold lettering.

Any magic you can do, I can do better.

March 29th

6:00

K

114

Reed laughed, the sound tinged with admiration. The wizard gave a bow amidst applause and whistles and then departed. Many glances were cast about as Reed's classmates sought to identify who was the intended recipient. Reed just sat in his seat, staring at the letters until the annoyed professor erased them.

As the professor droned on about brain chemistry and behavior, he couldn't extinguish the smile on his face. He still didn't know what to do with Kate, but the prospect of another date sent excitement burning in his chest. She'd sent the invitation.

And he would answer.

Chapter 21

Reed drove home in an excitement induced euphoria. Kate had asked him out. And she'd done so with all the creativity and cleverness he could hope for. Jackson and Shelby were sitting at the table. Both turned at his entrance, and both looked smug. Reed shut the door and put down his bag before turning on them.

"We had a visitor in class today," Reed said. "You wouldn't know anything about that, would you?"

"It's possible we received a request regarding your class schedule," Jackson said, scrunching his face up as if attempting to remember.

Shelby tried to suppress a smile and failed spectacularly. "I hear some think psychology is magic."

"Just whose side are you on?" Reed asked.

They exchanged a look and chorused in unison. "Kate!"

"Traitors," Reed muttered.

They dissolved into laughter. Although he feigned anger, Reed was actually grateful for their betrayal. Kate would not have been able to pull off such a clever date invitation without assistance, and to be on the receiving end was exhilarating.

Over the next week he tried to stay focused on his classes, but Kate dominated his thoughts. When it was his turn to ask he'd made a point not to call, and told himself it was for her benefit. After all, he couldn't afford to give her the wrong idea.

But as much as he tried to convince himself that it was for her, he'd refrained from calling out of fear. What was rapidly becoming an unspoken tradition of not calling left him feeling decidedly unsettled, and he frequently found himself staring at his phone, wondering if she'd call.

Despite his conflicting thoughts he looked forward to the following Thursday. He'd received no further contact from Kate since the invitation and had no idea what to expect on the date. Although he was tempted to anticipate and come prepared, he realized he could inadvertently ruin her plans.

He laughed at himself when he realized he was thinking so much about Kate that he'd all but forgotten other dates. Several were still on the calendar but only one between the invitation and the date.

The girl's name was Willow. She was on the dance team, so he took her dancing. It was a different location than where Kate had shown him, a place he felt reluctant to share with someone else, but he frequently thought of Kate. The moment Willow realized he could dance, her perspective changed, and she was clearly attracted to him. When he declined her invitation to come into her house after the date ended, she was disappointed, but all he felt was relief. He drove home wondering just how much Kate had changed his life.

The rest of the week passed in a blur, and by the time Thursday night rolled around he struggled to keep his excitement in check. Jackson took notice of his fidgeting and provided a constant flow of comments about Kate. Giving up on doing homework, Reed threw a ball of paper at Jackson and went to get ready.

"Don't fall in love with her!" Jackson called brightly.

"I won't," he cast over his shoulder.

He shut the door on his room and sank onto his bed. It had been three years since Aura, but the ache had yet to subside, and he'd begun to wonder if it ever would. He'd never spoken to anyone about what had happened, and only his sister knew the whole truth.

He reached into his wallet and pulled out the picture he hid in the back pocket. Holding it aloft, he looked at Aura's smiling face. He stared at it until he could no longer bear the regret, and then returned it to his wallet.

Vacillating between regret, worry, and excitement, he stood and got ready for the evening. Choosing jeans and a comfortable button up shirt, he brushed his teeth and then stepped into the living room.

Mercifully, Jackson was occupied preparing his nightly bowl of cereal, and Reed took the chance to slip to the door and depart. Jackson called out as he left but Reed pretended he didn't hear. Shutting the door, he sat on the stoop.

It had begun to rain, the storm bringing sheets of water upon Boulder. Rivulets of rain coursed down the driveway to merge with the current in the gutter, the sound a soft patter that filled the street. The door opened behind him and Jackson sat next to him. He didn't speak, and instead munched on his cereal in silence.

"You're a loud chewer," Reed said. "Did you know that?"

He snorted and spoke through a mouth of Golden Grahams. "Shelby may have mentioned it."

Reed grunted. "She is always honest."

Jackson continued to chew, the sound matching the rain. They sat watching the storm for several minutes but neither moved. When it became clear Jackson was not going to leave, Reed threw him a look.

"Is there something you need?"

"Can't a friend enjoy the rain with a friend?"

"No."

Jackson glanced his way and shrugged. "Normally you're excited about a date, but you're acting like me after I lose a game."

"I'm fine."

Jackson waited a moment and then looked his way. "Just make sure you don't hurt this one," he said.

"I'm not going to hurt Kate," he said, a little heated.

"Good," Jackson said, unperturbed. "Because it's the ones we truly care about that we hurt the most."

118

"Did you get that on a fortune cookie?" Reed asked.

"Maybe," Jackson said. "Look, you're the best dater I've ever known, but we both know you keep your distance. You need to be careful with this one, or you're going to regret it for the rest of your life."

Reed released a long breath, his anger dissipating. "Do you think I should end the challenge?"

"Of course not," he said with a bark of laughter. "I think you've found the one you've been looking for."

"I wasn't looking for anyone."

"I know," Jackson said. "But you've still found her."

Reed raised an eyebrow. "Since when have you been the dating master?"

"Since I had a fortune cookie," he said.

Reed grinned. "I'll try to be careful."

"Good," he said. "And can you pick up more cereal? We're out."

"What kind of person eats cereal for dinner *every day?*"

"The kind with taste," he said, shoveling another spoonful into his mouth.

A car appeared at the end of the street and Reed recognized it as Kate's. Rising, he waved to let her know she didn't need to come to the door in the rain and then turned to Jackson. His roommate was also on his feet and now leaned against the porch post.

"Have a good time," he said.

"I will," Reed said, and then added, "And thanks."

Just as Kate's car came to a stop, Reed jumped off the porch and raced through the rain to the passenger door. Pulling it open, he stepped into the car and shut the door. Then he turned to Kate, his words dying on his lips.

Dressed in a black robe and a scarf of blue and bronze, Kate also had a pointed hat on her head. She smiled as she endured his scrutiny. Then she reached to the back seat and retrieved a robe, scarf, and hat for him.

"Just where are we going?" Reed asked.

"Didn't you guess?" Kate asked, her green eyes shimmering with delight.

Reed examined the black cloak and then the red and yellow scarf. Although he'd only seen a few of the movies, he recognized the clothing as belonging to Gryffindor. Wrapping the scarf around his neck, he held the hat aloft.

"Harry Potter?"

Her smiled widened. "You're a wizard, Reed."

Chapter 22

"You have no idea how long I've waited to hear those words," Reed said fervently.

"When I turned twelve I stayed awake all night waiting for my owl," she said. "I was heartbroken when it didn't arrive."

"Little kid problems," he lamented.

They shared a grin, and he stole a look while her attention was on the streetlight. Her green eyes sparkled with amusement and excitement, and he suddenly realized the concerns of the last two weeks were gone. The moment he'd stepped into the car his worries had evaporated.

He stole another look and realized that right now the reasons didn't matter. He may not have made his choice, but in this moment, all he wanted was an evening with Kate. Resolving not to think about Aura the rest of the night, he turned to face her.

"How did you ever get your wizard friend to do your invitation?"

"He is Brittney's ex," Kate said.

"And he agreed to do her a favor?"

"Not at first," she said. "But then Brittney unleashed Ember, and he didn't last long."

Reed smiled at the image of the diminutive redhead berating the poor guy until he agreed. He may have been a wizard, but no amount of magic would protect him from Ember. Still, he appeared to have enjoyed the opportunity to perform a trick.

"He was flawless," he said. "Did you like planning the invitation?"

"Enormously," she admitted. "Although it was difficult coming up with ideas. The best person to ask was the one person I couldn't."

"Perhaps," he said. "But you did pretty well on your own."

"You think so?" she asked.

He heard a trace of nervousness in her voice and smiled. "Like I said, flawless."

She smiled. "I'm still getting used to creative dating. It's fun, but it takes more time than I thought."

"It gets easier," he said.

"Does that mean it was hard for you at first?"

"It was," he said.

"What was your first date like?"

"I was sixteen—"

"So late?" she asked with a smile. "I assumed you started dating in grade school."

"I was actually pretty shy until late in high school," he said. "I also had enough acne my face looked like the surface of Mars."

"Really?" she asked. "You look great now."

"Don't patronize me."

She laughed. "Seriously. I think the word Marta used to describe you was 'dreamy.'"

He raised an eyebrow. "I think that's a bit much."

"I think you grew up good," she said, a touch of pink appearing in her skin.

Uncomfortable with the attention, he said, "I didn't actually date much in high school. It wasn't until my second year here that I started dating like this."

"What changed?"

"I just got tired of waiting," he said with a shrug, hoping he didn't sound evasive.

"Everyone is waiting for the right one to come along," she said. "But that doesn't explain how you started to date like this. What was your first creative date like?"

"A disaster," he admitted. "I tried to do a breakfast date but the girl didn't eat carbs. The breakfast was homemade waffles."

She laughed. "So you started doing research?"

"I adapted," he said. "And like I said, it gets easier." He suddenly realized they were staying close to campus. "So what's this date you have planned?"

"Why do you ask when you know I won't tell?"

"Perhaps I'm just hoping we're going to Hogwarts."

Her smile was smug. "You'll see."

He'd expected them to travel off campus, but instead they returned to her house. The other cars were absent from the driveway and she parked close to the front door. They ran through the rain to the porch and caught the door handle. Her smile was excited but nervous as she swung the door open. He stepped on the threshold and came to a halt, stunned by the transformation of the room.

Sheets made to look like stone covered the walls, while flickering candlelight glimmered in brackets. A golden snitch made of paper hung in the corner, spinning and twirling above a strategically placed fan. Books had been wrapped to look like spellbooks, the one on the corner table labeled *Hogwarts, A History*.

Other candles hung from the ceiling from barely visible fishing line. Although plastic, they glimmered like real floating candles, casting the room in a spooky light. A sign above the kitchen had a crooked arrow beneath the words *To Hogsmead*.

A cauldron sat on the kitchen table, smoke bubbling up from the interior and flowing off the table to dissipate above the floor. Plates on the counter contained what appeared to be treacle tart and cauldron cakes. A bag had a note marking its contents as Bertie Bott's Every Flavour Beans.

The table had the main course, including a salad and corned beef sandwiches. Next to the table, the TV had been set on the floor and showed a roaring fire, the flames crackling on the screen. Boxes had been painted like bricks to resemble a hearth.

"It's stunning," he breathed.

"Welcome to Hogwarts," she said.

He spared her a look and found her veritably bouncing on her feet with excitement. It was abundantly obvious that she'd spent the entire two weeks preparing the room, and likely enlisted the help of her roommates—as well as anyone Ember had coerced into helping—to finish by tonight. The sheer volume of effort was both impressive and humbling, and he offered a short bow.

"I tip my hat to you, good witch."

She pulled him through the room, pointing out every detail. He admired each in turn before she led him to the table for dinner. As he took a seat she dipped a ladle into the cauldron and filled a cup.

"Butterbeer?"

"I assumed it was root beer," he said, peering into the smoke.

"Nope," she said. "Brittney wanted it to be authentic, so she put a pitcher in the middle with dry ice, and then filled the rest with butterbeer."

"Clever," he said.

"She actually did all the cooking," Kate admitted. "I'm a decent cook, but I would have needed a wand to do what she did."

He laughed and sipped the butterbeer, which tasted deliciously like caramel. Throughout the meal he continued to praise both the decorations and the food. By the time they moved on to desserts they were sitting on the floor in front of the fire.

He nibbled on the cauldron cake, which tasted like hot fudge wrapped in a warm brownie. Savoring every bite, he sampled the treacle tart while polishing off another glass of butterbeer. She enjoyed the food just as much, and sighed as she licked chocolate from her fingertips.

"You missed a spot," he said, reaching out to brush a streak of fudge off her cheek.

The motion made her flush. "Thank you," she said.

His touch had been instinctual—yet pushed against his rules. Surprised by his own action he covered with a smile. There was an awkward moment of silence and then he spotted the bag of Bertie Bott's Every Flavour Beans.

"Are those real?"

"Actually, they are," she said. "Brittney bought them on her trip to Orlando and ate two. Then she refused to eat another."

"What were the flavors?"

"She swears they were band-aid and blood."

He grimaced. "Do we dare brave them?"

"I will if you will," she said. "But you first."

He grabbed the bag and selected one that looked like chocolate, but turned out to be burnt toast. She laughed at his expression and then chose a green one, which she announced was evergreen.

Choosing another color, Reed said, "I can't believe you pulled this off." He swept his hand at the room.

"I liked your idea of a theme," she said. "And when I was trying to come up with one I was in my room."

"I remember your posters from St. Patrick's Day," he said.

She cocked her head to the side. "You know, you're the only non-boyfriend that has been in my bedroom without me."

He grinned. "I hope I didn't leave it too messy for you."

"Actually, it was quite messy," she said, and then flashed a smile. "But if you're not careful, you're going to make my roommates fall for you."

"I did warn you about dating like this," he said. "Spend this much time on a date," he swept his hand at the house, "and the guy will think you *really* like him."

"Perhaps I do," she said with a smile.

His heart thumped in his chest and he covered by throwing a bean at her, making her laugh. "Don't think you've won this competition yet," he said. "We're just getting started."

"Oh are we?" she asked, throwing a bean back at him.

The ensuing Bertie Bott's Every Flavour Bean War lasted for several furious seconds until they ran out of beans. Laughing, they set about cleaning it up and then returned to the table. Once there, he refilled her butterbeer and she nodded her gratitude.

"I hope you've enjoyed Hogwarts," she said. "But we still have the activity."

"There's more?" he asked.

Her eyes sparkled with amusement. "Of course. Are you ready for more?"

He understood the secondary meaning but could not resist the answer. "Always."

Chapter 23

They exited the house and made their way to the car. After all the effort to decorate the house, he'd expected the activity to be inside Hogwarts, but instead they got in the car and headed to downtown Boulder.

"Where are we going?" he asked, unable to contain the question.

"Are you always so demanding of your dates?" she teased.

"Yes."

She smiled and shook her head. "When you give answers, I will."

It was after eight and traffic was light, but as they entered the downtown area it became progressively more congested. Even on a Thursday, the downtown clubs were packed. Passing them by, she entered the lot of the large downtown mall and found an empty parking spot.

"Do we need to remove the robes?" he asked, pulling at the wizard's robes.

"Nope," she said. "We'll fit right in."

They exited the car and made their way through the rain soaked lot to the mall. Reed expected people to stare at their clothing, but the moment they stepped inside it became clear that they were not alone.

Hundreds of people were dressed in Harry Potter garb. Most were in robes, but some were dressed as wizard-muggles, with one boasting a purple suit and top hat. Others wore outrageous combinations, and wands were in abundance.

Children in robes rushed about, pointing wands at each other and shouting spells. Teenagers wore scarves of various houses and huddled in groups whispering and laughing. They passed a group and Reed noticed they were holding lists for a scavenger hunt, each specific to the Hogwarts houses. Then Reed spotted the giant banner hanging from the rafters.

Diagon Alley

March 25-30

Reed leveled an accusing finger at Kate. "You are far more clever than I anticipated."

"This is date number four," she said, delighted by his response. "I figured you expected an easy win and I wanted to dissuade you of the notion."

"When did you hear of this?" he asked, motioning to the mall.

"I actually didn't until yesterday," she admitted. "I had planned a different activity but when I learned of this I couldn't resist. It wasn't very well advertised."

"It's certainly well attended," he replied, gesturing to the wizarding crowd.

"Word got around quickly," she said. "And Marta heard it from one of her cousins, who works at Cold Stone," she pointed to a restaurant that now had a sign for *Florean Fortescue's Ice Cream Parlour*.

Other shops were also changed, and the mall now contained Eeylops Owl Emporium, Flourish and Blotts, Gringotts Wizarding Bank (formerly US Bank), and of course, the Leaky Cauldron. The Gap had become Madam Malkin's Robes for All Occasions.

Reed looked about himself in wonder. Every shop was giving away Harry Potter themed candy and treats, with some doing drawings for clothing or real wands. Children dressed in wizarding robes lined up at the bookstore where they were given bookmarks and entered into drawings for books, movies, and cauldrons.

The playground in the mall had been turned into Hogwarts. Kids crawled in and through the castle, their squeals of delight adding to the din. To Reed's surprise, many of the parents were also dressed up, some apparently choosing specific characters. A Professor McGonagall was so perfect, the wizards she passed called her by name. Another wore stilts and resembled Hagrid, right down to the beard.

Kate turned into the bookstore and threaded her way through the crowd. Harried workers rushed about, but there were smiles on their faces. They too were dressed in robes, most in black but one in garish orange, another in lime green.

Kate came to a halt in the fiction section of the bookstore. "Ready for the game?" she asked.

"I already own the Harry Potter books," he said.

She shook her head. "We each have nine minutes to read a book, but the book is chosen by the other. We have three minutes and forty seconds to pick out a book. Then we start anew."

"Nine and three quarters?" he asked.

"Of course."

He laughed. "Any book?"

"Any in the bookstore," she said. She pulled out her phone and set a timer. "Clock will be ticking, so don't be late—and try to choose books you actually like. It's supposed to help me know more about you."

"Which roommate came up with this game?"

"Marta's mother," she said.

"I'm starting to feel very understaffed in this competition."

She grinned. "You have the advantage of experience. I needed my own advantage."

"At least you can admit who is better."

She snorted and tapped her phone. "Go!"

He darted away and hurried down an aisle, scanning for books that were familiar. As packed as the store was it was difficult to navigate, and he had to slip past groups of browsing shoppers. Stepping into the fantasy section, he worked his way down the row until he found some of his favorites.

He guessed they would only have time to choose a handful of books for each other, so he didn't just want to pick any title. Passing some of his favorites, he opted for a Terry Brooks title from when he was a kid. He reached their meeting point just seconds before she did, and they exchanged books.

"*The Night Circus*?" he asked, raising the book.

"One of my favorites," she said. "Be glad I didn't get you *Twilight*."

"Don't assume I won't like it," he said. "Perhaps I like vampiric romance."

"Actually, I think you like epic fantasy," she said. "The Elfstones of Shannara? I've never even heard of it."

"Then you've missed out."

The phone went off and they found a pair of empty chairs in the corner. Settling in to read, he was highly conscious of the fact that Kate was just a few feet away, and found himself apprehensive as to her verdict on the book. He also enjoyed the introduction to a new novel, and when her phone rang he was disappointed.

"This really isn't fair," he said. "You're going to make me blow my weekly budget on books."

"Did you read a lot as a kid?"

"I did," he said. "But I didn't have much else to do. To be honest, I only had one true friend till my sophomore year of high school."

"What was his name?"

He hesitated, and then said, "Aura."

"A girl?" Kate asked, pausing in resetting the timer on her phone.

"I met her in third grade and we were close friends until college."

"You were friends for a decade and then it just ended?"

He shrugged. "She met a guy."

"That does have a way of ending friendships," she said.

Jumping at the chance to shift the topic back to her, he said, "You sound like you're talking from experience."

She smiled. "Perhaps. Ready for the next round?"

They started the clock and then went again. This time he picked a Percy Jackson novel. She returned with Twilight. They both laughed and settled in to read. Nine minutes later he held the book up to her.

"It's better than I thought it would be," he said. "But nine minutes isn't enough to decide if I like it."

"I thought it dragged a little in book two, but book four was a lot of fun. Are you going to buy it?"

"Shelby has a copy," he said. "I'll borrow it from her." He smiled at the image of Shelby's expression when he asked to borrow Twilight.

For the next hour they exchanged books, trading genres and titles like they were baseball cards. He liked some, but not all of the books she gave him. He was surprised when she brought a Jack Reacher book, and he surprised her with a book on M.C. Escher. Then the books became more amusing.

She brought a yo-yo trick book, while he returned with a coloring book on Star Wars. Moving outside the fiction section, they began choosing gun magazines, short stories, even game strategy guides. They still read, but their reading time quickly dissolved into laughter as they told stories about why they'd chosen their books.

Reed relished his time with Kate, but avoided any topic that might lead back to Aura. Several times he caught her giving him a measuring look and wondered if she'd noticed his evasiveness. When it became clear they were no longer reading, she gave up on the game and they returned the books they didn't want. Reed stood in line with four new books, including *The Night Circus* and *Cinder*. Kate had three.

"I used to read with my grandmother," Kate said as they waited in line.

"The one living with your dad?"

Kate shook her head. "My grandmother on my mom's side. My family would visit her in California every Christmas and we would read by the window. She's the reason I love to read, and she even bought me my first Harry Potter book."

He noticed the softening in her tone. "You sound like you had a good relationship."

She nodded. "She was funny and crass, but she loved me. She passed away three years ago."

"I'm sorry."

Kate shrugged, her eyes looking past him. "Her bout with cancer was hard, so I couldn't be too mad when it ended."

"I used to go camping with my grandfather," Reed said. "He taught me fishing and backpacking. He was really into boy scouts before and after World War II."

They reached the front of the line and paid for their books, and then vacated the space for a group of girls buying posters of Cedric Diggory and Victor Krum. Exiting the store, he motioned to the mall.

"It's only 9:30," he said. "I hope we aren't leaving the Wizarding World of Harry Potter just yet."

"We still have the treat," she said.

"An after-date treat?" he asked. "Are you following my manual?"

"Of course not," she said with a laugh. "I'm *improving* your manual."

Chapter 24

As they walked down the mall he shook his head. "You think you've won this round?"

"I would say quite handily."

He chuckled dryly. "I won't admit to that—but I will say I like your magic."

They entered Florean Fortescue's Ice Cream Parlour and ordered, and then took the only available seats. The crowd had begun to diminish with the hour and the lines had dropped off. Reed guessed it would be even busier on Friday and Saturday, so he was glad they'd come today.

She'd gotten butterbeer and a bowl of mint chocolate chip with a waffle cone on top. He'd gotten the same, and for several minutes they talked about the books they had purchased. Then Reed recalled that they were supposed to play a different game.

"Are we not telling stories of our worst dates?" he asked.

"That was my original plan," she said. "But how could I pass up taking you to Diagon Alley after Hogwarts?"

"I was hoping to win that game," he lamented.

"Next time it's my turn," she promised.

He grinned and sipped his butterbeer. "I look forward to it."

She regarded him for several moments, and then said. "Can I ask you a personal question?"

"Of course."

"Are you okay?"

He raised an eyebrow. "Why would you ask that?"

She shrugged. "I don't know. Tonight you just seem . . . reserved."

He thought of Aura and shook his head. "I'm fine."

"Every once in a while you smile, but it doesn't quite reach your eyes."

"Have you been watching my eyes a lot?"

A shade of pink lightened her skin and she nibbled on the waffle cone. "Maybe," she admitted.

He kept a smile on his face but inwardly he struggled. Few of his dates had been perceptive, but Kate seemed to read him as easily as she had the books in the store. He found it disconcerting yet strangely freeing to have someone notice what he hid behind a smile.

"Do you read everyone so well?" he asked.

"No," she said. "Just you."

He laughed without humor, and then on impulse said, "Remember Aura?"

"The girl that was your friend?"

"You remind me of her."

"Is that a bad thing?"

He shook his head. "On the contrary. She was the best person I knew."

"Then thank you?"

"Really," he said. "No matter what happened, I could count on her to be there."

"So what happened?"

"Like I said, she met a guy and we stopped being friends," he said.

"Just like that?"

"It took a couple of years," he said, "but she just kept drifting away. She didn't even tell me his name for a long time. I tried to stay in touch but I think she thought I was jealous."

"Were you?"

"Yes," he said with a smile.

"So you *did* have feelings for her."

"I did," he replied. "I would call her my first crush, but I never told her how I felt."

"How exactly do I remind you of her?"

"Aura had your courage," he said.

She stirred her ice cream. "I don't feel brave."

"You've challenged Michael Jordan to a basketball game—and are winning. My grandfather would have said you have moxy."

She laughed. "So you're Michael Jordan?"

"And you're winning."

Her smile was smug. "Creative dating is not at all what I'm used to."

"What were you used to?"

"A club, a bar, or a movie theatre," she said. "That sums up most of my dates. And I count myself lucky. For most of my friends, dating consists of casual sex followed by a lack of texting and sometimes regret."

"The idea of being single has changed," he agreed. "My grandfather used to curse about the degradation of society."

He filled his spoon with his ice cream, idly wondering if the conversation had shifted on its own, or Kate had shifted the topic on purpose. With how perceptive she was, he couldn't be sure. She seemed at ease, but he suspected the topic would come up again, and wondered what more he would say.

"It's odd," she said, her expression going distant. "This sort of dating makes me think of my grandmother—the one in California—but she would be very disappointed to know I was the one asking a guy. She believed it was the boy's duty to ask, and the girl's duty to shoot him down."

"What was her husband like?"

"That grandfather died when I was little," she said. "But I felt like I knew him because of my grandmother. She called him a little firecracker."

"Little?"

"He was five feet tall."

"Little, then," he said with a laugh. "Mother's side, right?"

"Mom," she said. "He was a colonel in the army."

"You said your parents were divorced, but they still get along?"

She nodded. "Thanksgiving we all get together."

"All of you?"

"Yep," she said. "And yes, it's weird, especially now that my dad remarried."

"You have a stepmother?" he asked.

She laughed. "I call her Debbie, and she's not too bad."

"And she gets along with your mom?"

"They're polite," she said. "But they're not friends."

"I hate what divorce does to families," he said.

"My mom thinks that our culture doesn't allow marriages to last anymore."

"What do you think?" he asked, scooping the last of his ice cream.

She shrugged. "I think she's right—to a point."

"What do you mean?"

She finished her butterbeer and sat back, her expression turning pensive. "I don't think couples know how to last, so they don't."

"Is that what you want?"

"I know I don't want to go through what my parents did," she said. "They called it amicable, but I called it torture. I never knew what tore my family apart."

"I hated what my dad did to my mom," he agreed.

She smiled and gestured an invitation. "What kind of husband would you be?"

"Is this an interview?"

She laughed and shook her head. "Seriously, you know how to date, but what would you do with a wife and family?"

He pushed his empty bowl away, giving himself a moment to consider his answer. "I don't know. I think dating like this would be impossible when married, when there are kids and a job involved." He shrugged. "I wouldn't want to stop, though, so I guess I'd have to be even more creative."

She began to chuckle, a wry amusement that caused the remaining customers in the shop to glance their way. He raised an eyebrow, but she merely shook her head and pointed at him. Then she leaned in.

"We talked about marriage and you're not running."

He snorted. "Of course not. I'll run after you drop me off."

They shared a laugh and then rose to discard their bowls. The shop and mall had emptied while they'd enjoyed their ice cream, with only a few stragglers making their way towards the exit. Reed spotted a clock and realized it was nearly 11, and the mall would be closing soon. He hadn't realized how long they'd been talking over ice-cream, and he marveled at the ease of their conversation.

"I guess it's time to return to the muggle world," he said.

"Don't be so disappointed," she said. "At least you got to be a wizard for a day."

"I have my work cut out for me on our next date," he said. "But I think I have a few surprises up my sleeve."

"My roommates are certainly on your side," she said as they made their way towards the exit.

"I think both our roommates are loyal to the *date*," he said dryly. "They don't care who's asking, they just want to be involved in the secret."

"I'd say that's entirely accurate," she said. "Ready for our picture?"

He smiled and they posed under the banner. A kind Dumbledore offered to take their picture and fumbled with the phone like he was really an aged wizard. When they were finished they walked out to the car.

"Any advice on working with Ember?" Reed asked. "I'd like to know how to use her in my next covert operation."

She grinned as she pulled out her keys. "Don't make her angry. She's like the Hulk in a tiny redheaded body."

"I'll keep that in mind."

They got into the car and she drove through the empty streets. The rain had slackened and was hardly a drizzle, barely wetting the windshield. As she pulled into his driveway he unbuckled the seatbelt.

"Is there a surprise waiting in my bedroom?" he asked.

"Not this time," she said with a smile. "But you get to keep the robes."

"Really?"

She smiled. "I thought you'd like a memento of your visit to Hogwarts."

"It was magical," he said.

She laughed and exited the car, coming to the other side to open his door. Then they walked to the porch. He stole a look as they passed under the porch light. She'd removed her hat before leaving the car and rainwater sparkled in her hair, her green eyes were as bright as ever. He'd dated many beautiful girls, but Kate surpassed them all.

"You're beautiful, you know that?"

"Do you say that to all your dates?"

"It's true," he said, catching her arm to bring her to a halt. She glanced at his hand in surprise and he removed it. "It's true," he repeated quietly.

A soft smile appeared on her face. "Goodnight, Reed. Until next time."

"Until next time," he said.

She embraced him and then walked to the car, waving farewell before shutting the door. He remained on the porch and watched her go, wondering what he was getting himself into. And if he could get himself out.

Chapter 25

Jackson appeared at Reed's side as Kate drove away. "How was Hogwarts?"

"How much did you know?" Reed asked.

"All of it," he said. "I must admit, I really like playing for the team against you."

"You're back on my side now, right?" He glanced Jackson's way to gauge the reaction.

"So you've decided to keep going?"

"I like her too much to stop," he said.

Jackson smirked. "So you admit it?"

"Just don't tell anyone," he said. "It's hard enough to hold to my rules as it is. I can't afford to let word get to her."

"I promise," Jackson said.

"So you're on my team?"

"Only for the next two weeks," he said. "Then we go back to her side."

"*We?*" he asked, turning to him.

"Her roommates, Shelby, me, and a few others."

Reed laughed sourly, realizing his assumption had been more accurate than he'd thought. "You're like a team of spies," he said, stepping to the door and swinging it open. "What's your agenda?"

"To get you together," Jackson said.

"No one asked you to do that," he snapped.

Jackson stopped, his smile fading as Reed rounded on him. "I thought you liked this girl."

"I do," Reed said. "But there are things you don't understand."

"Then enlighten me," Jackson said, stabbing a finger at him. "We're trying to help you."

"I don't need your help," Reed said.

Reed turned and escaped to his room, grateful he had the sense not to slam the door. Then he sank onto the bed and stared at the ceiling. On impulse he picked up his phone and clicked on Kate's number. Then he began to type.

I'm sorry, Kate. I can't do this anymore. Please don't ask why.

His thumb hovered over the send button, but he couldn't bring himself to do it. After several seconds he released an explosive breath and jammed his finger down on delete, erasing the message. Then he tossed the phone aside so he wouldn't be tempted.

Kate didn't deserve such an ending, not after everything she'd done for him. She liked him, that much was obvious, and she was playing his game. If he quit now he would never forgive himself.

When he was with her he felt free of the burden that had plagued him for three years, but when she was gone that weight returned, a crushing mantle that he'd grown accustomed to wearing. He sighed and pulled out Aura's picture. Was he betraying her? Was he betraying his promise? Or would she be happy with his competition with Kate? But the picture had no answers, and he put it aside to avoid the reminder.

The minutes dragged by and he half expected Jackson to knock on his door. Reed rarely lost his temper, and never with Jackson. The fact that Jackson didn't knock suggested he didn't know how to respond, and was likely talking to Shelby now, hoping she knew what to do.

He fleetingly considered telling Jackson the whole truth about Aura, but chances were he would just tell the blondes, and then Kate would know. Then the whole dating challenge would be over anyway. He sighed and rolled over, his thoughts turning to memory.

He thought of Aura's smile, her defiance when other kids picked on him. Of her fawning over Tim when he'd called. He thought of her changing in the next few months, and the years they'd gradually drifted apart. Then he remembered her final call.

And how she'd lost her life.

Part 5: The Island Date

Chapter 26

Kate and Marta parked outside the restaurant, *Carne Asada*. Owned by Marta's uncle, the restaurant was Brazilian, and several of Marta's cousins worked there, as well as Marta's mother. The moment they walked in the door Maria engulfed Marta in an embrace.

"Mi hija!" she cried. "You do not visit enough!"

"I work here," Marta said, extricating herself with a sigh. "I'm here every week."

The large woman snorted and shifted her attention to Kate, pulling her into an equally effusive hug. Kate smiled at Maria, grateful for the boundless love the woman possessed. She hugged everyone, and everyone was family.

The restaurant wasn't large but it was renowned for its unusual blend of Puerto Rican and Brazilian cuisine. Pictures and flags of both countries were on proud display, while the décor boasted steer horns and other rancher equipment.

She shouted to one of Marta's cousins and he prepared a table. Once they were seated she fussed over Marta, pulling at her hair and speaking half in English, half in Spanish. Marta finally snapped in Spanish and the woman threw her hands in the air. Muttering to herself, she turned to Kate.

"How's the dating challenge?"

Kate wasn't surprised she knew about Reed. "It's his turn," she said. "But he hasn't asked yet."

"Why are you asking him at all?" Maria asked. "He's supposed to be chasing you."

"It's just a game," Kate said with a smile.

"Then make sure you win," Maria said.

"*Mother*," Marta exclaimed in surprise.

Maria blew out her breath and walked away to greet the next customers. Her muttered words were in Spanish, and Marta rubbed her forehead wearily. Kate's smile turned sympathetic and she lowered her voice so Maria wouldn't hear.

"She does love you," Kate said.

"I know," Marta said. "But my family can be stifling. She doesn't understand why I'm going into Nursing when I could get an accounting degree and work here."

A young man overheard the comment as he walked to the table with a couple of glasses. "Because you *don't* want to work here," he said with a smile.

"Hector!" Marta exclaimed, rising to greet her brother. "I didn't know you were working today."

"Just filling in," he said.

Hector was expected to play soccer, the sports his dad had played, but much like Marta, he had his own dreams. Unfortunately, he was still in high school, so Maria required him to play baseball as well. He frequently had to skip basketball practice because their family didn't think it was important.

He was already tall for his age, and his dark complexion and dark eyes were a lethal combination for the girls. Maria had banned several from the restaurant because they would come just to watch him work.

"So how's Reed?" Hector asked.

Kate shot Marta a look. "Just how many of your family know about him?"

"All of them," Hector said. "And most of the customers by now."

"Mom won't stop talking about it," Marta said.

"So will you help me?" Kate asked, turning to Hector.

145

"I'm always on your team," Hector said, and then smiled. "Except when it's his turn."

Kate laughed dryly. "I find it disturbing how quickly my friends betray me."

"Get used to it," Hector said, clearing the table next to them. "We're just glad you're not moping about because of Jason—"

"*Hector!*" Marta snapped.

"Sorry," Hector said. "Let me know when you're ready to order."

Kate waited until he was gone, fighting to control her emotions. Marta started to speak twice but ultimately fell silent. Kate had hardly thought of Jason for weeks, but it appeared Marta had been telling her family a great deal.

"I love your family," Kate said tightly. "But I don't like being the source of your family's gossip."

"I'm sorry," Marta said. "I told Hector everything, but no one else. And he would never share it with anyone."

It was a consolation, but not a big one. Still, she couldn't expect her roommates to hold every secret. She sighed and nodded, and Marta looked relieved. Once they'd placed their order, Marta leaned back in her seat.

"What's wrong, Kate?"

"What makes you think anything is wrong?" Kate asked.

"You've been on edge for the last week. Did something happen on your Hogwarts date?"

Kate shook her head, and then on impulse said, "The date was fine, but something about Reed was off."

"In what way?" Marta asked.

"I can't put my finger on it," she said. "We had a great time and he clearly enjoyed everything, but there were several times I noticed an odd expression, like his mind was elsewhere."

"That's not a good sign," Marta said. "You think he's losing interest?"

Kate jerked her head. "I don't think it has anything to do with me. I can tell he likes me—more than he wants to admit, actually."

She smiled as she recalled him touching her arm when she'd dropped him off. His touch was nothing, hardly necessary, but his expression revealed his own surprise. He *wanted* to be close to her, but his habits held him in check.

"So what does it have to do with?"

"Can you keep a secret?" Kate asked. "And I mean from Ember, Brittney, and your family?"

Marta nodded, and Kate didn't doubt her. Of any of her roommates, she trusted Marta the most. She may have told her brother about Jason, but she'd never broken Kate's confidence when specifically asked not to.

"He mentioned a girl named Aura," Kate said.

"Past girlfriend?"

"No," Kate said slowly. "She was his best friend for years but he wanted more. Then something happened and it was over. When he talked about her there was a tightness to his smile that I'd never seen before."

"You've only been on four dates," Marta said. "Do you know him well enough?"

"I think so," Kate said. "He's very open, but with Aura I think he's holding back."

"Everyone has their secrets," she said. "Are you going to push him on it?"

Kate shook her head, still uncertain. She wanted to know what Reed was hiding, but not for herself. She sensed that whatever had happened had left a scar, and she felt a yearning to alleviate that pain. Before she could speak further their meal appeared and Hector set the steaming plates on the table.

"Let me know when you're ready for dessert," he said, and then disappeared again.

As they ate their dinner, Kate noticed Marta checking her phone. It was the third time she'd done so since they'd entered the restaurant. At first Kate suspected she was waiting for a guy to call, but then realized Marta was purposefully keeping the screen away from her.

"What's Reed doing while we're here?" she guessed.

"How should I know?" Marta asked, flustered by the straightforward question.

"You were quite insistent that I come to dinner with you," Kate pointed her fork at her. "Just tell me, am I going to like the surprise?"

Marta sputtered for an answer and then gave up. "You're going to *love* it."

Heat warmed Kate's chest, spilling into a smile. "He may be hiding something, but he can't hide what he feels for me."

"I wish I had a guy to ask me like this," Marta said wistfully.

"I'm asking him too, you know," Kate replied. "There's nothing stopping you from doing the same."

"Yes there is," Marta said, and threw a meaningful look at her mother, who was seating a family nearby.

Kate smothered a laugh. "How would she react if you asked a guy on a date?"

"She would disown me," Marta said. "I'm already breaking her heart by living away from the house and doing Nursing. All she has left is setting me up on blind dates with guys from Puerto Rico."

"At least she's trying."

"My last date breathed through his mouth like a leaf blower," Marta said. "He could have cleaned our steps just by walking to the front door."

"It couldn't have been that bad."

"The people in the movie theatre thought the air conditioning was broken."

"Was he at least cute?"

Marta stabbed her steak. "No. He wasn't."

Kate began to laugh but turned it into a cough when Maria walked by. Marta was beautiful, but her mother was insistent she go on dates only with others from the island. It gave Marta an excuse to avoid other guys, but she still had to date the ones her mother approved of. With how many cousins she had, word eventually got back to her mother that she'd dated someone else.

They finished their meal laughing about Marta's past dates, and by the time they were in the car Kate's thoughts turned to what evidently awaited her. Knowing an invitation for their fifth date was coming soon caused her to fidget nervously.

"Trust me," Marta said. "The guy is like a dating savant."

"He is rather brilliant," she agreed.

Marta threw her a long look. "Are you sure you want to fall for him? He may not want anything more than the game."

Kate had no answer. "For now," she said, "that's all I want too."

I think.

Chapter 27

Kate noticed Marta's expression and frowned. "I know what I'm doing," she said.

Marta grunted, the sound infused with doubt and amusement. Her expression and tone matched her mother's inflection so perfectly that Kate grinned. She pointed back to the restaurant.

"I thought your mother stayed at the restaurant," she said. "But I hear her voice in the car."

Marta's eyes widened in surprise, and then narrowed. "Please don't say I sound like my mother." She shuddered. "You'll bring my nightmares to life."

They shared a smile and then Kate attempted to glean information about Reed's latest invitation. Marta proved surprisingly resilient, refusing to provide even the tiniest detail. Resigned to wait, Kate tried to guess based on where they were going, but Marta turned down the road towards home.

"Really?" she asked. "I expected something a little more."

Their dinner had been late and the sun was already setting. The streetlights were on and the horizon glowed a dull orange. As they pulled up to the house, Kate saw that only Ember and Brittney were present, both talking outside Ember's jeep like they had just gotten home. But their posture was too excited, their attention too focused on Kate's arrival.

"They're terrible at pretending," Kate said.

"We're new to being spies," Marta said with a smile. "I'm sure we'll get better with practice."

They pulled into the driveway and Kate exited. Ignoring Ember and Brittney's feigned surprise, she strode to the door and swung it open. The darkened interior of the house greeted her. Nothing was different.

She frowned and looked back at her roommates. They stood together on the driveway, their anticipation brighter than the streetlights. Confused, Kate took a step inside and peered around in the darkness. There were a few dishes from lunch in the kitchen sink but nothing out of the ordinary. Then she spotted a large paper ball on the floor. In the dim light she noticed holes in the paper but could not tell if they were letters, numbers, or symbols. Intrigued, she reached for the light switch, but paused.

There were two switches on the wall, one to the ceiling light, one for the lamps. The arrows pointed to the second switch. Then she noticed an extension cord running from the wall to the ball in the center of the floor.

She flipped the switch and light blossomed inside the paper ball, cascading out of the holes to shine on the walls and ceiling. She'd expected letters and text, a message of some kind, but instead they were stars. Reed had turned her home into the night sky.

Kate stared in wonder. The timing had been perfect, with the fading light of day allowing the light in the room to truly shine. She stepped into the room and turned a slow circle, marveling at the flawless display.

"Well?" Ember demanded from the open door. "Aren't you going to say anything?"

"It's stunning," Kate breathed.

"Reed arrived just after you left," Brittney said. "He set it up remarkably fast."

A smile spread on Kate's face as she gazed on the starry room. Reed had done all this, for her. He'd meticulously cut out stars from the covering and probably placed it with care. Game or no game, heat suffused her frame at how much time he'd spent on her.

"Where's the invitation?" she asked, her eyes still on the host of stars. Then she realized the stars were not shining on blank wall. She stepped to the corner of her couch and leaned in to see a Starburst candy highlighted by the star, held to the wall with tape. She scanned the room and realized other stars were also position to fall on pieces of candy. "Does it have to do with this?" she asked.

"He wouldn't say," Ember said. "He said you'd have to figure it out on your own. Although he was very particular about the placement of the Starbursts, so I'd suggest we start there."

Kate noticed they all whispered, even Ember, as if reluctant to disturb the scene. Marta was as enthralled as Kate, and stared at the walls, her eyes reflecting the starlight. Together, all four began searching the stars, and they worked their way around the room, hunting for clues. Five minutes went by, then ten. Kate retreated and examined the shapes of the stars but found no clues in the shapes. They attempted dimming the light, but that didn't reveal anything. Then they each took a wall and examined it up close. As Kate shifted from star to star, she noticed one Starburst was not lit by a star.

She frowned and reached for it, wondering if Reed and made a mistake. Her fingers stopped a hairsbreadth from touching the dark starburst and she smiled. She squinted and looked at the dark wall, and began to spot the others.

"Some of the candy doesn't have a star," she exclaimed.

"So he just made a mistake," Ember said with a shrug. "I saw a few of those."

Kate looked over her shoulder. "Did he put the Starbursts up with the stars on? Or off?"

Ember frowned. "On. But why would that matter . . ."

"Take down any candy lit by a star," Kate said.

"Why?" Brittney asked.

Kate pointed to the wall. "With the stars on, he wouldn't miss one. I think he placed candy in the darkened sections where the stars *don't* touch."

She hurried to a wall and began removing all the Starbursts that were touched by a star. Then she took a step back and pulled out her phone.

"Brittney, turn off the light."

She stepped to the switch and cut it off, plunging the room into darkness. Then she flipped the second switch for the overhead light— but it didn't come on. In the darkness Brittney giggled.

"He took out the bulb," she said. "I don't think he wanted it to be that easy."

Laughter reverberated in the gloom as Kate pulled out her phone and turned on the flashlight, turning it on the nearest wall. She gasped when the remaining Starbursts were shaped into words.

I'd be over the moon,

With the secret revealed they rushed to clear the other walls, and then they all pulled out their phones. Ember protested when Marta's light shined in her face, and then they turned the lights on the walls to read aloud.

"I'd be over the moon," Kate said.

"If my date you'd be," Marta said.

"For a night of stars," Brittney continued.

"And wonders to see," Kate finished.

Kate turned her flashlight to the ceiling, which revealed the date and time. She began to laugh and her roommates joined in, all four delighted at finding Reed's clues. Then Kate turned the stars on again and they stood in the magical room.

"Well we know one thing," Ember said.

"What's that?" Brittney asked.

"Kate's in trouble," she said smugly.

Kate grinned with the others. She knew Reed had a talent for creating romance, but this felt like more than a game. She turned a slow circle, her heart fluttering as she gazed on the twinkling stars, hoping it was not her imagination.

They left the lamp on the floor and turned it on each night. Word spread to friends and neighbors, and girls flocked to the room to see the starry invitation. Kate found herself the center of a great deal of attention and speculation. Even Marta's mother stopped by after work. Dressed in her uniform from the restaurant, she stood in the center of the room, marveling at the stars on the walls.

"Your next invite had better be perfect," she finally said.

"Mother!" Marta exclaimed, her voice tinged with surprise.

"I'm not as old fashioned as you think, daughter." Marta stood in shock as Maria embraced Kate. "And bring him to dinner," she said. "I'd like to meet him."

Laughing at Marta's shock, Kate embraced the woman and then walked her to the door. Marta joined her on the threshold and watched her mother walk to her car. Only when she was gone did Marta speak.

"Reed hasn't even met her, but he's changing my mother."

"I can't believe she *wants* me to ask Reed out," Kate said.

"She loves you like a daughter," Marta said.

"She loves everyone like a daughter."

"True," Marta said with a laugh.

Kate glanced her way. "Does that mean you're going to start this creative dating?"

"I just might," she said in amusement. "I'm tired of waiting on guys who have no initiative."

"You might chase them away," Kate said. "I doubt all guys can handle such a modern woman."

154

"Doesn't matter," she said. "If they can't handle the evolution of dating, they aren't worth pursuing."

They shared a laugh and shut the door. Then Kate went to her room and struggled to finish her history paper. She managed to finish late and sat back with a sigh. For several minutes she stared at the screen of her laptop.

She was surprised to realize just how much her life now revolved around her dates with Reed. It was just their fifth date, but she thought about him every morning, during class, and when she got into her car. Everything was an idea for a future date, and everything harbored potential for the next invite. Reed was rapidly becoming the center of her world. But she couldn't shake her nagging doubt.

Chapter 28

Reed arrived promptly at 6:30, his knock drawing Kate and her roommates to the door. Other girls and a handful of guys were in the living room. Ostensibly there for a movie night, they were really there to see Reed arrive.

The girls were curious while the guys were irritated. Kate overheard enough of the conversation to know the wistful talk by the girls did not sit well with the guys, who apparently felt the weight of their girlfriends' rising expectations.

The knock at the door sent a hush through the room and Kate rose to answer. When she swung it open Reed's eyes swept the room, a faint smile crossing his face as he spotted the girls gathered to see him. His black hair combed, his blue eyes sparkling with amusement, he was attractive and inviting.

"Movie night is better with sound," he said.

One of the girls fumbled with the remote and turned the sound up, causing a round of giggles and laughter. The guys looked annoyed. The blondes were amused.

"You've met him," Kate said. "Now enjoy your movie."

More laughter ushered them outside and only ended when the door shut. "Sorry about our friends," Kate said. "Your invitation drew a great deal of attention."

"I don't mind," he replied. "But the guys didn't seem too happy."

"You're making their girlfriends think they're not doing enough," she said.

"Are they?"

"Probably not," she said wryly.

They climbed into the car and it groaned to life. As they pulled onto the street, Kate frowned as she noticed several faces peering through the window. It might have been jealousy, but she found the increased attention irritating.

"Have your dates ever garnered attention?" she asked.

"Sometimes," he said. "But I try to avoid it."

"Your stars certainly drew them in."

"Stars are always magical," he said. "And after your invite last week, I needed to show you how it's done."

She smiled at his teasing tone. "The invite was good, but we'll see about the date."

He flashed his easy smile, the expression that was rapidly becoming her favorite. Then he turned down the street that led to his house. Guessing the destination, she raised an eyebrow and pointed towards his house.

"Going home?"

"Your last date was flawless," he said. "It's only fair I return the favor."

"And the theme is stars?"

"Like I said," he replied, "they're magical."

She sniffed. "We'll see."

He smiled but did not respond. As he turned up his street she stole a look, wondering when her life had begun to revolve around him. His lack of communication between dates left her uncertain, but all the concern faded away when she was with him, and she marveled at the boldness that he elicited. He glanced her way and caught her looking.

"What?" he asked.

"I just look forward to our dates," she said.

"Me too," he said. "But how could I not?"

"I bet you say that to all the girls."

He laughed. "Not many girls to say it to now."

The words settled in as he pulled into the driveway and put the car in park. "I thought we weren't exclusive," she said.

"We aren't," he said. "But I haven't had much time of late."

He glanced her way and then changed the subject, but she noticed a seriousness to his blue eyes, as if he wanted to date her—and only her. The prospect thrilled her, forcing her to look away so he wouldn't notice her smile. By the time he'd come around the car to open her door she'd managed to rein in her emotions.

"Hungry?" he asked.

"Starving," she said.

"Good," he said. "Dinner is this way."

Instead of going to his house, he turned toward the neighbors and threaded his way between the houses to the backyard. She spotted the light first, but as they rounded the corner she blinked in surprise.

White Christmas lights extended between the house and the back fence, bathing the backyard in soft light. Instead of grass, most of the backyard was dominated by a large pool. The white Christmas lights reflected off the pool water, making it seem to dance and shift.

Crossing the pool, several long beams supported a platform at the center, where a table and two chairs hovered over the water. A pair of lit candles further illuminated the white tablecloth, plates, and a bowl of bread at the center.

"This is incredible," she breathed, making her way towards the table.

"Welcome to an island under the stars," he said, sweeping his hand at the display. "I would say it's deserted, but you'll have to share it with me."

She smiled as she placed an experimental foot on the path to the island. "I'll make do."

He laughed and followed her to pull out her seat. Made of plywood, the island was not ornate, but the dinner table was. Fine china and silver utensils were perfectly laid out, and the smell of warm bread implied it had just been placed. She reached for the bread and brought it to her nose, breathing deeply of the intoxicating scent.

"When did this come out of the oven?" she asked.

"A few minutes ago," he replied. "My assistants departed just before we arrived."

"And your neighbors just let you build an island on their pool?"

"He's let me use his backyard before," Reed said, "but this time he had a price—that he gets to use the island for a date with his wife tomorrow night."

Her smile faded as she imagined Reed sitting across the table from a host of other girls. Reed looked up from pouring olive oil into a bowl and noticed her expression. Confusion washed across his features as he added parmesan and spices to the bowl. Then abruptly he smiled in understanding.

"I've never done anything like this, though," he said. He gestured to the dangling lights and the island on which they sat. "Not for any other girl."

She grunted in irritation. "Am I that easy to read?"

"Let's just say you are a subject matter I enjoy studying."

She laughed and dipped her bread into the bowl before taking a bite. She closed her eyes at the taste, which recalled dinner at a fine restaurant. It may have been with Jason, but she found him easier to dismiss than ever.

"This is incredible."

"I'm not the best of chefs," he replied. "But I have a handful of dishes that I can do to satisfaction. Fortunately, Jackson is better than I."

"Doesn't he eat cold cereal for dinner?"

"Every day," Reed said. "But this time I managed to convince him to share his culinary skills."

"What does he get in return?"

"I plan a date for him and Shelby."

She laughed, imagining Jackson taking Shelby on a Reed inspired date. Over the last few weeks she'd talked with Reed's roommate on several occasions, and he'd proved a willing accomplice in her endeavors. Kate had also spoken to Shelby, who was certainly willing to jump into the conspiracy.

"I see the Italian theme," she said, gesturing to the olive oil and the bread.

"It's a safe bet," he replied. "Everyone likes Italian. Ready for the salad?"

She shook her head. "I'm happy with an infinite supply of the bread."

He laughed and left the table. Making his way to his neighbor's back door, he slipped inside, and a moment later returned with two plates of Caesar salad. Complete with croutons and tomatoes, it perfectly resembled restaurant fare, except it lacked . . .

"Parmesan?" he asked, lifting a grinder over her plate.

"Please," she said with a smile.

He covered her salad with cheese until she stopped him and then added some to his own. Then he returned to his chair and began to eat. As they ate she pointed to the island, wanting to know if he'd spent too much.

"All borrowed," he replied. "My neighbor is a builder, so he lets me use surplus wood as long as I return it relatively undamaged."

"Did he help you build it?" she asked. "Or should I worry about it crumbling?" She feigned trepidation as she looked at the water.

"I had help," Reed said.

"This is truly magical," she said. "But what would you have done if it rained?"

"I have a backup," Reed said. "But it's not nearly as good."

"Few things compare to an island under the stars," she said.

"You took me to Hogwarts," Reed said. "Least I could do was take you to Italy."

She sat back in her chair. "I thought I had you beat," she said.

"Just wait," he said, his blue eyes dancing in the candlelight. "The night is young."

Chapter 29

They progressed from salad to the main course, chicken fettuccini alfredo. It was delicious, but her attention remained on Reed. The privacy and enchantment of their makeshift island was like a scene from a movie, and she frequently had to pause to calm her fluttering heart.

A warm spring breeze floated across her skin, but she shivered at the intensity of the moment. Lights reflected off the pool, sparking, shimmering, and dancing across the table, highlighting Reed's smile. With darkness surrounding the backyard they were alone in the world.

"Tell me something," she said, finally pushing the plate away. "Did you ever plan creative dates for a girlfriend?"

He cocked his head to the side. "What do you mean?"

She swept her hands to indicate the date. "You said you'd had two girlfriends, neither of which was serious. I want to know if you put this much effort into the relationship *after* you were already together."

"I stopped shaving and showering," he said. "It's just so much *work*."

She laughed. "Seriously. What did you do for your girlfriends?"

He leaned back in his chair and used the napkin to wipe his lips. "My girlfriends were prior to my dating, so not much, but not for lack of desire. One relationship lasted only a few months, while the other was even shorter."

"Really?" she asked. "Who ended it?"

"One me and one her," he said. "Let's just say that expectations were not met."

She smiled, recalling that he was still a virgin, and his girlfriend may not have liked that. She'd hoped that talking about his girlfriends would bring up Aura, but either by intent or accident he didn't mention her.

"I'm surprised they aren't stalking you."

"How do you know they aren't?" he asked with a smile.

"You're cute," she said, "but without your superpower you're just a normal guy."

"So you admit I'm cute?" he asked. "I'm flattered."

"I don't recall saying that," she said, stifling a smile.

"Too late," he replied. "The words are cemented in memory."

"I also said you were normal."

"I don't recall that."

They shared a laugh and then she leaned in. "When I was little, my parents used to go on a date once a month. They would go to a restaurant and leave me and my brothers with a babysitter. We were terrible and none of the babysitters lasted long."

"But they still went?"

She nodded. "They used to talk about date night like it was the most important thing in the world, like without it our family would crumble, but over time their dates gradually became infrequent. Then they stopped entirely. Looking back I wonder if I was witnessing the gradual decline of their marriage."

"What do you think caused the decline?" he asked.

"My mom always denies it, but I think it was us," she said, looking at him but seeing her parents arguing. "They gave so much attention to me and my brothers, there wasn't much left for each other. Then one day they sat us down and said he was moving out. I was angry but also relieved."

"You were relieved they were splitting up?"

"They'd been arguing for a long time," she said. "And I remember avoiding the house to avoid them. When he moved out it came to an end, and they stopped trying to force something that was gone. Then things got better."

"You said you hated that they split," he said.

"I hated having a divided family," she said. "And even though they were happier, my brothers and I despised going between the two houses, and the feeling of being torn. I blamed my mom for a long time."

"You shouldn't," he said, "at least not entirely. Relationships require constant work to maintain, and couples that don't put in the time see it wither and die."

"How would you know?" she asked, smiling to take any sting from the comment. "You've never had a serious relationship."

"Perhaps," he allowed. "But it seems pretty obvious, doesn't it? What you make a priority thrives, what you neglect, dies."

"I don't think they meant to neglect each other."

"They probably didn't notice it happening," he said. "But you said yourself they paid a lot of attention to you and your brothers. I suspect if they had focused more on each other, they might still be together."

She looked away, realizing that although he didn't have the experience, his words sounded true. Her thoughts turned to Jason and she wondered what a life with him would have been like. It wouldn't have been earth shattering, but they would have stayed together, if only because he loved her. Their dates may have been mediocre, but he'd sought time with her whenever possible, and he'd been devoted.

She frowned as she recalled Reed's major. "Are you using psychology on me?"

"I would never do that," he said, and then smiled. "Maybe a little."

"That's not really fair," she said. "You have psychology and what do I have? Engineering."

"You could tell me if the island will support us."

164

She stomped her foot on the boards and watched the water ripple away, bending the lights reflected on the surface. The sight brought a smile to her face as she once again felt the enchantment of their date.

"Don't worry," she said. "I don't hold a grudge against my mom anymore."

"Good," he said. "Because she's proud of you."

Kate raised an eyebrow. "Now how would you know that?"

"I talked to her this last week," he admitted. "I had a question only she could answer, and Marta gave me the number."

Kate studied Reed with new eyes. "I knew we were recruiting allies, but I didn't realize our families were free game."

"I thought you'd be mad."

"That the guy I'm not dating called my mother?" she asked with a smile. "Why would I be mad? I bet she was thrilled."

"She did seem excited," he mused.

"I bet she was surprised."

"That too."

She laughed, imagining her mother getting a call from a guy she would immediately assume was her boyfriend. No doubt she'd grilled him like a steak on the barbeque, but Kate was surprised she hadn't called. Apparently anticipating her question, Reed smiled.

"I asked her not to call you until after tonight."

"Then I should block out most of the day tomorrow," Kate said ruefully. "She'll want every detail, and there's a lot to share."

"It's only been five dates," he said.

"Five dates with you is the equivalent of a hundred with a normal guy."

"I'll take that as a compliment," he said, flashing his easy smile.

Kate privately decided that his smile was also unfair. She was certain he knew its impact, and used it to great effect against her. Not that she minded. Then he glanced at his watch and rose to his feet.

"Dessert is later," he said, clearing the table. "Ready for the activity?"

"I don't really want to go," she said, rising to help.

"We aren't going," he said, his blue eyes sparkling. "The activity is right here."

She glanced at the pool. "The water's too cold to go swimming, and I didn't bring a suit."

"We aren't going swimming," he said.

Rebuffing her attempts at answers, he cleared the table and chairs, and then took down the table. Then he retreated to his garage and returned a moment later with a roll of padding and a few quilts, which he laid out on the island. She laughed as he assembled what could only be described as a mattress.

"No hand holding, and now we're jumping into bed?"

He laughed in turn. "No touching, I promise."

"Then what's with the bed?"

"It's a viewing island," he said.

"For what?" she asked. "The sky?"

He grinned, his silence providing a confirmation. Then he gestured to one side and reclined as well, leaving a conspicuous gap between them. When she was comfortable she looked to him, her lips twitching in amusement.

"Sure you don't want to push some boundaries?"

He shook his head and smiled. "You should take this as a compliment. I trust you enough to lay down a short distance from you."

Her laughter washed across the backyard and she wiggled to get comfortable. Then she looked up at the lights and waited expectantly. He withdrew a remote and pressed a button, and the lights abruptly winked out.

She sucked in her breath as they were plunged into darkness, and blinked repeatedly to get her vision back. As the lights faded the stars appeared like diamonds on velvet, twinkling in the moonless sky.

"So we're going to watch the stars?" she asked.

"Not exactly," he said. "You mom said you've never seen a shooting star."

"So?" she asked.

"So," he said, gesturing to the wide expanse of the sky. "I hope you enjoy your first meteor shower."

A chill swept across her skin as she turned back to the sky, her breathing accelerating as she gazed upon the infinite expanse. With no cloud to mar the view, the millions of stars became the show, and with each passing second her heart thumped faster. Then a streak of light flew across the sky, brief yet stunningly beautiful.

"Make a wish," he murmured.

Chapter 30

She clapped her hands in delight as she watched another meteor streak across the sky. The sight of a celestial object elicited a sense of wonder and excitement, drawing another shout when one appeared from another angle.

"This is incredible," she said.

"It always is," he said.

'You've done a meteor shower with someone else?"

"Will you stop comparing your dates with others?" he asked, his voice amused. "I promise I will never repeat anything I've ever done with another girl."

"Was that so hard to say?" she asked.

"Not really," he said. "You've thrown down a challenge, and I find my previous dates just don't meet the same standard."

"I still think I can win."

"Not after tonight," he said.

She wanted to disagree, but another meteor appeared. "Don't get comfortable with your lead," she said.

She could almost hear his smile but he didn't respond, and for several minutes they just watched the sky. After the initial burst of meteors nothing appeared, but she was in no hurry. In that moment it was just her with Reed, gazing up on a magical sky. When another meteor appeared she released a sigh.

"I've always wanted to see one," she said.

"That's what your mother said."

"How did you know to ask her?" Kate asked.

"You'd be surprised how many people haven't seen a shooting star," Reed said. "It was a gamble, but moms usually know."

Kate shot him a look. "You've called other moms?"

"Only those I know best," he said. "I avoid it because it builds a certain expectation."

"I almost saw a meteor shower in August a few years ago, but it was cloudy," she said.

"The Perseids," he said, nodding. "They're one of the best. This is the Lyrids."

"Are there usually this many?" she asked, pointing to one appearing to the east.

"Actually, this isn't the ideal night for the Lyrids," he said. "But it was the only night that the forecast said would be clear. Sunday would be the best."

"I'm running out of wishes," she said, as another shooting star appeared and flared to life.

"Tell me one of them."

"That means it won't come true."

"You can always re-wish it," he said.

She hesitated, and then decided he was right. "I wished for a new computer."

"I wished for my car to survive."

"I think it's already dead," she said with a laugh.

"It's still moving," he protested.

"Like a zombie," she said, "and about as fast."

Another star appeared and lasted the longest yet, eliciting a murmur from both of them. A pair of meteors followed in quick succession, and for several seconds they just enjoyed the show. When another lull came he chuckled.

"I wished for a job after I graduate."

"When do you graduate?"

"The end of this year," he said.

"Then what?"

"One of my old professors took a job in New York. Their practice is quite prestigious and they take a few paid internships each year. With his recommendation I was accepted."

"You never told me what type of psychology you're interested in."

"Can't you guess?" he asked. "Marriage and family."

She burst into a laugh. "Going to teach husbands to date their wives?"

"It's what my thesis is on," he said.

"Really?" She threw him a glance and then returned her eyes to the sky, unwilling to miss another star.

"Jackson and a few friends agreed to be case studies," he said. "I planned their dates and they told me the impact."

"And?"

"Too early to tell," he said. "I just started, but Shelby has thanked me profusely."

She smiled at the image of Jackson executing a creative date. She wondered if the creative dating would have a lasting impact on their relationship or would it flare and fade like the shooting stars.

"Do you think he will continue to do creative dating?"

"Not to this extent," he said, "but he doesn't do bar dates anymore."

"How much of that is Shelby's influence?" she guessed.

"A lot," he said, his tone amused. "She told me in one of our interviews that he'd upped his game, and she wouldn't let him go back to the minors."

"She deserves it," Kate said with an approving nod. "I've gotten to know her a little and she's great."

A trio of meteors appeared and disappeared, and they fell silent, both awed by the heavenly display. More flashed across the night sky, the sight eliciting a deep yearning within Kate. On impulse she said what she'd really wished for.

"I wished this night would never end."

"Why?"

"Isn't it obvious?" she asked softly.

He didn't answer, and she stole a look. When they'd first laid down his hands had been on his chest, well clear of her, but now his hand was close to hers. She swallowed, recognizing it as a tiny push against his boundaries. As casually as she could, she laid her hand down on the blanket a short distance from his.

The space between them was just inches, but it sent tingles up her hand. She swallowed, wondering if this was the moment—hoping this was the moment. She saw a shooting star and wished for his hand to close the gap.

"I've never enjoyed a night so much," he murmured.

"Is it me or the date?" she asked.

"Both," he admitted.

She glanced at his hand. Was it closer? Or was it just her imagination? She couldn't be sure, and almost missed the next meteor. She swallowed at the sudden dryness of her throat, wondering why she was so nervous. The last time she could recall feeling so desperate to hold a boy's hand was Jimmy Bell in the fifth grade. But Jimmy wasn't nearly as attractive.

Highly conscious of the feel of the fabric beneath her fingers, she drifted her pinky closer. Their hands were now so close she could feel the heat from his hand, and imagined his palm wrapping around hers, of the lightning it would send up her arm. Just then a flurry of meteors burst across the sky as if the heavens anticipated this very moment. Gathering her courage, she tensed her muscles and . . .

Her phone rang, the sound so jarring they both jumped. She fumbled for her phone and pulled it from her pocket, silencing it without looking at the caller. It could have been the president and she wouldn't have cared.

She laughed at being startled. "Sorry," she said.

"No need to apologize," he said. "I took my phone out already because I nearly fell in the pool when I was building the island."

He rapped the island with his knuckles to emphasize his point . . . and returned his hand to his chest. She winced and looked away, unable to keep her disappointment from her face. Had it all been her imagination? Or had he come a hairsbreadth from breaking his rule?

"Ready for the dessert?" he asked.

Forcing a smile, she turned to him. "What's for dessert?"

He rose to his feet and she did as well. "Italian Gelato," he said. "I'll be back in a minute."

He smiled and strode up to the back door of the neighbor's house. The moment he was gone she turned away and released a muttered curse. Her disappointment turned to anger at her phone, so she pulled it from her pocket and turned it to silent before stuffing it into her purse. Even though she doubted another opportunity would arise tonight, she couldn't risk it.

Reed appeared and walked to her with two bowls in his hand. It seemed to her that he walked slowly, as if giving them time apart. He stepped onto the bridge and strode to her.

"Raspberry or—"

In the darkness his foot caught on the edge of the padding and he tripped. The bowls went flying past her and she instinctively reached to catch his hand, but in her haste she stepped too close to the edge of the island. She caught his arm. She didn't catch her footing. She cried out as she pulled Reed into the pool.

Chapter 31

They plunged into the freezing water and went under. It was the shallow end and she twisted to come to the surface, bringing her head above water and gasping for breath. It was April in Colorado in an unheated pool, and the cold pierced her clothing like a thousand frozen needles.

"I'm sorry!" she chattered. "I didn't mean to pull you in!"

Shaking a few feet away, he grinned. "I'm sorry for lying."

"When did you lie?" she asked, pushing her way to the edge of the pool.

"I said we weren't going swimming."

Freezing, shaking, and desperate to leave the pool, she burst into laughter. He reached the edge first and pulled himself out. Then he helped her to the edge. Shaking and wrapping her arms around her chest, she followed him back to his house.

"You need to get out of those wet clothes," he said, his teeth chattering.

"You might take advantage of me," she said through chattering teeth.

He managed a laugh and led her into the bathroom, where he turned on the water and put a towel on the sink. She stood in the center of the bathroom, shivering and dripping wet, but unable to remove the crazy grin on her face.

"Straight to the shower?" she asked. "No cuddling?"

He grinned. "Not today. I'll find a bag for your wet clothes."

"What about you?" she asked, her whole body shaking.

"I'll dry off and change," he said, his smile marred by his own shivering. "Take your time."

He exited and shut the door, and she quickly stripped and stepped into the shower. The blissfully hot water coursed over her body, gradually taking the sting from the pool. She stayed until steam filled the shower and the heat seeped into her frozen bones, and then reluctantly exited and dried off. Just as she finished wrapping the towel around herself there was a knock.

"I've got the sack for your clothes."

"Come in," she said brightly.

"Are you covered?" he asked suspiciously.

"You'll just have to trust me," she said.

He swung the door open and extended an arm with a sack. She reached out and pulled the door open, revealing Reed in new clothes, a coat, and a beanie. He also had his other hand covering his eyes. She grabbed the sack.

"I'm covered," she said.

Apparently deciding to trust her, he peeked an eye open and then smiled at her in the towel. "Better?"

"Much," she said, withdrawing clothes from the bag, which proved to be pants, a thick thermal shirt, and a belt.

"Jackson didn't have a bra?" she asked.

"I'm afraid his wouldn't fit," he said.

She laughed and gestured to the door. "I'll be out in a moment."

She shut the door and then dressed in his clothes. She had to cinch the belt to keep the pants from dropping, but at least she was warm and dry. Rubbing the towel through her hair, she stepped into the living room to find him sitting on the couch under a blanket.

"I was still cold," he admitted.

She stepped to the couch and he lifted the blanket so she could slide under. Wiggling to a spot at his side, she shivered beneath the heavy quilt. Although the shower had taken the sting, the chill remained.

"Do you think you can break your rule for the sake of warming me up?" she asked.

"Just this once," he said, and wrapped an arm around her shoulders.

His motion was careful, but she leaned against him with a grateful sigh. Neither of them spoke, and for several minutes they just enjoyed the return to warmth. She noticed he placed his hand with great care and found herself grateful. She'd been on dates where the guy let his hands wander, and it was a relief not to have to worry about Reed. She relished the sensation of security his arms provided.

The minutes ticked by but he didn't seem inclined to move, and they talked of stars and the meteor shower. When their hands had almost touched she'd felt a magnetic pull of attraction, but now it was a pure comfort, like being wrapped in the warm blankets they gave you at the hospital. She smiled faintly and closed her eyes. After a while Reed shifted.

"Sorry you didn't get the dessert," he murmured.

"I'm not really up for a cold dessert," she said.

"It's about time to go," he said, using his chin to point to the clock. "It's almost midnight."

She groaned. "Do I have to go?"

He smiled and shifted, lifting the blanket so they could separate. They pulled away and she exited the warm cocoon to gather her things. As he grabbed his keys and phone, he froze and whirled to face her.

"Your phone!"

"I took it out before we fell in," she said. "It's probably still in my purse on the island."

"Were you *planning* on dragging me in?"

"What if I was?" she asked as they walked outside.

"I would have worn a swimming suit," he said.

The partial moon had risen while they were inside but the stars were still bright. With one of Reed's jackets to ward off the chill, she followed him back to the island. He picked up the bowls and spoons discarded onto the grass and then entered the neighbor's house. She stepped onto the island and retrieved her purse, turning her gaze to the heavens.

He joined her and rolled up the blankets. Then he stood at her side. As if guessing her intent, he said nothing for several moments, waiting for a final shooting star. She sighed in satisfaction as it burst into life and then faded.

"Thank you," she said. "Tonight was enchanting."

"Even the swim?"

"Even the swim."

They shared a smile and then he walked her back to the car, pausing long enough to leave the roll of blankets in the garage. Then they climbed into the car and he drove her home, arriving just before midnight. He walked her to her door and gave her a hug.

"Your turn," he said into her ear.

"It will have to be good," she said.

"I'm confident it will be," he said, pulling away. "Goodnight, Kate."

"Goodnight, Reed."

She watched him walk to his car and then entered the house. When she opened the door a flurry of movement signaled there were several people in the room and she clicked on the light switch. Like deer caught in headlights, the light revealed the blondes trying to escape from where they'd been spying at the window. They looked her up and down, taking in the view of her in his clothes.

Ember recovered first. "Did you—"

"No," Kate said. "We fell in the pool."

"Pool?" Marta asked.

She sank onto the couch and quickly narrated the events of the date. Her story suffered countless interruptions as her friends *ahhed* over the romantic moments. Her description of them almost holding hands elicited a round of laughter, and when she came to the part where they fell into the pool Brittney was shocked.

"Was he furious you pulled him in?"

Kate cocked her head to the side. "You know, he wasn't."

She hadn't realized it at the time, but he'd responded with humor when he could have easily blamed her for a mistake. Instead he'd eased the tension and reacted quickly under pressure. Marveling at his response, she nearly missed Ember's next question.

"How did you warm up?"

"I used his shower," Kate said.

"And he never touched you?" Marta asked. She sounded disappointed.

Kate smiled. "He put his arm around me to help me stay warm."

Ember folded her arms. "I don't know if I should be disappointed or happy for you."

"Happy," Kate said with certainty. "I really like him."

Brittney pounced on the statement. "We knew it!"

Kate endured their triumph with a soft smile. Then Brittney offered hot chocolate and they all accepted. Several minutes later Kate sipped the delicious heat, grateful that the warmth in her chest still lingered from his arm around her shoulders.

"Wait," Brittney said. "When you were about to hold his hand, who called you?"

"I assumed it was one of you," Kate said.

All three shook their heads in unison, and Kate reached for her purse. Pulling out her phone, she opened it and froze, her eyes fixed on the text message that had followed the call. She didn't hear her roommates until their queries became more ardent. Then she finally looked up.

"It was Jason," she said, stumbling over the words. "He's coming back to Boulder and wants to meet."

Part 6: The Dare Date

Chapter 32

In the week after their starry date, Reed wondered if he'd gone too far. Kate had become a dominating presence in his thoughts. He went to class and work, but she was there, her face, their hands almost touching, her smile when they stood in the pool, her in a towel after her shower.

He swallowed and forced his attention back to his homework. Opting to study in the library instead of his house, where Jackson and Shelby were constantly talking about him and Kate, he found a seat at one of the tables in the large study area.

The library filled all three floors of the building. Stacks of books lined the interior while a bank of windows looked out onto the sunlit grass. Computers were on the second and third floors while the first contained desks and chairs, many of which were occupied. The sound of students discussing group projects was a welcome hum. Reed turned the page and tried to read about the chemicals in the brain that contributed to certain psychiatric disorders.

What about Kate made her so arresting? He wanted to call her, to be with her, to see her smile. His classes, even the ones he liked, had become a chore, a distraction from planning the next date. Even though it was her turn, he kept thinking of what he could do next, with each idea becoming more extravagant than the last. As he considered his options, he surveyed his surroundings, wondering when her next invitation would come.

Growing bored with his textbook, he sat back in his chair and looked around the library, smiling and nodding mechanically at the girl behind the counter, who he'd taken on a date several months ago. She was a short brunette with a perfect sense of humor, and their date had been clever and fun. She'd described it as a pinnacle of her single life, and initially showed interest. When it became evident the relationship would not progress she'd accepted it well, and they were still friends. Molly smiled and nodded back, and then she returned her attention to her book, her expression annoyed. He guessed she was working on her physics homework, which she hated with a passion.

He sighed and returned his attention to his book. His professor liked to surprise his students with a quiz every Friday. The surprise was gone after three weeks and the students came prepared. Realizing he was reading the same paragraph, he rubbed his face and leaned back again. For what felt like the hundredth time he tried to solve the enigma that was Kate.

She'd matched him date for date, stepping into the creative dating with an ingenuity that surprised him. She didn't just try, she triumphed. He smiled as he recalled her exiting the pool, her expression apologetic yet amused.

A clatter of metal drew his attention to the doors, and he spotted a member of the band entering, dressed in his uniform and carrying a trumpet. While not strange in itself, he was followed by the rest of the band. Whispers and smothered laughter followed as the group continued to file into the library and fall into formation, bringing their instruments to their lips.

The librarian spotted them and rushed over, her urgent hiss for quiet going ignored. More and more came in through the door and stood against the wall. All marched in place, their eyes fixed on the drum major as an expectant hum filled the library. Drawn to the disturbance, students appeared between the bookcases as the drum major stepped to a place between tables and raised his hands.

Reed braced himself for a blast of music, but instead the song was incredibly quiet. Titters of laughter came from the students as the full marching band attempted to play within the quiet confines of the library. Even the drummers were muffled, barely touching the drumsticks to their drums as they kept time.

At first Reed assumed it was a stunt from the band, perhaps orchestrated by a fraternity for their pledges. But as the band played and the librarians hissed their dismay, he caught numerous looks in his direction, and realized the band was there for him.

A smile spread on his face as he witnessed Kate's handiwork. The band's effort to keep quiet was well executed, but occasionally an instrument blasted a note, causing the entire library to erupt into stifled laughter, eliciting the ire of the head librarian, Miss Sturges.

The elderly woman loved the library more than the students, and many had been on the receiving end of her infamous glares. She made even the football players scurry away like frightened mice, although she was a third their size.

She stood several feet from the drum major, attempting to quell the marching band's uprising by force of gaze alone. She nearly succeeded, but the combined might of a hundred and fifty students huddled together and armed with brass instruments proved too much for the old woman, and they continued to play.

"I never thought I see someone best the Sturg," a student nearby murmured.

"The band will probably be banned," another said, eliciting smiles and groans in equal measure. Someone threw a ball of paper at the speaker.

Reed sat listening to the muffled song, his smile undiminished. He'd used the stars and she'd returned with force, somehow enlisting the entire school band. How had she done it? How did she convince so many to show up for such a stunt? Or perhaps the better question was, who had her forceful roommate, Ember, terrified into assisting?

He snorted as he wondered who would win between Miss Sturges and Ember. One had a glare hard enough to bend steel, while the other possessed a look of fire that would melt said steel.

Reed noticed Molly shifting at her desk and glanced her way. She stood, enjoying the spectacle like everyone else. But every time the Sturg looked at her, she pretended intense annoyance. After three full minutes of quiet playing, the song came to its conclusion, and the banner bearers entered the room. Instead of their usual school colors, the banner displayed a question.

Brave a Dare?

Or Bare the Truth?

They walked about the room, weaving through the sea of desks and chairs, ignoring the questions cast at them as they marched back to the band. Then the drum major closed the song and began to file out. Undeterred by the Sturg's glare, the students erupted into quiet applause, their collective whispers a stamp of approval on the band, many of which broke character, their expressions showing triumph at their feat.

The whispers of praise and near-silent clapping came to a close, and Miss Sturges still hadn't moved. She folded her arms and rotated like a wrinkled cannon, unleashing the full might of her glare. The students resisted, but ultimately could not endure and gradually fell silent.

"You will respect this institution," she said, her voice somehow piercing the library to the corners, "or I will have you all thrown out."

She turned on her heel and strode away, leaving smiles in her wake. The students didn't dare raise their voices, but they whispered in huddled conversations, texting videos of what they'd witnessed to friends and reliving the moment.

Reed turned when someone stepped to his table, and found Molly leaning down. "She must really like you."

"How do you know that was for me?" he asked.

Her smile was condescending. "I'm not stupid. What number is this for you. Five? Six?"

"Does *everyone* know about our dating challenge?" he asked.

"You've dated hundreds of girls on campus," Molly said with a smile. "And I'm not the only to wonder who would finally snag you."

"You make it sound like I've been hunted."

Her smile widened. "Have fun on your date. Don't worry about telling me afterwards. I'll hear all about it."

"Are all my former dates in a club now?" he asked.

She merely shook her head and walked away, leaving Reed confused and excited. Realizing he would never be able to study now, he gathered his things and left the library behind. On his way home he wondered what exactly he'd unleashed.

Chapter 33

The night before their date Reed pushed through his studies, forcing a paper for one class while completing the research statistics for another. Then he rushed out the door to meet Jackson at Shelby's game.

The intramural program ran a fall basketball tournament and another in the spring, and Jackson and Shelby played in the men's and the women's leagues, as well as a co-ed team together. Shelby's team had managed to reach the finals and Reed had promised to attend.

Reed parked in one of the empty spots and hurried into the Coors Events Center. Due to the popularity of the intramural program, the final games always took place in the arena, and after a flurry of texts he managed to find Jackson close to the half-court line on the second row. He took his seat just seconds before the first whistle.

"You made it," Jackson said, sparing him a look.

"I promised, didn't I?"

With his entire face painted silver, and dressed in silver and blue, Jackson sat among the other hardcore fans. Shelby waved as she walked onto the court and took her place. Their team, the Silver Bullets, referenced a video game that both Jackson and Shelby liked, and explained Jackson's getup.

The whistle blew and the two teams fought for the ball, with the Disney Princesses coming up with it first. They dribbled the ball down as the Silver Bullets fell back onto defense, Shelby taking her position to guard the small forward.

"You've been distracted," Jackson said. "We would have understood if you couldn't—WATCH THE THREE!"

Jackson slipped into the bellow and then back to normal conversation with ease. After attending many events with his friend,

Reed didn't even blink. The guy next to him thrust a fist into the air when his girlfriend scored.

"We're taking them down, Jackson," he said.

"Not this time, Clint," Jackson replied.

Reed glanced at Clint. Dressed in full princess garb and a yellow wig, the tall ball player was clearly Rapunzel. He was also Jackson's friend and they were on the same team in the men's league. Reed always found it amusing that bitter rivals could be fast friends in sports—at least when they loved the game more than themselves.

"You look ridiculous," Clint said to Jackson.

"Look who's talking," Reed retorted. Both looked to Reed in surprise, and he realized he'd never joined in the trash talk. "Sorry," he said. "It's been a distracting week."

"How was the invite?" Clint asked.

"How do you know about that?" Reed asked.

"It made the school paper," he replied, and fished a newspaper from his backpack on the floor. "And it's on YouTube."

Reed accepted it and read about the band stunt in the library. It made no mention of Kate or Reed, but a picture of the banner and the invitation to a game of Truth or Dare was front and center—on the first page.

"This is getting bigger than I anticipated," Reed said, reading the article as Jackson crowed in delight at a Silver Bullet's play. His triumph was matched by Clint's dismay.

The article painted the stunt as Reed had suspected, as a prank by an unnamed fraternity or sorority. The author clearly knew nothing about the dating challenge, but it seemed everyone else did. Jackson and Clint were friends, so it made sense that Jackson had told him. Still, Reed wondered just how far it had gone.

"Why is everyone so interested in our challenge?" Reed asked.

187

"It's like you're an elephant in a city street," Clint said. "Everyone wants a look."

"Plus," Jackson said, "girls talk."

"Amen to that," Clint said fervently, causing a nearby boy dressed as Ariel to laugh.

"But this is getting out of hand," Reed said. "Molly at the library knew. I mean, how did she know?"

"Molly from six months ago?" Jackson asked. "I liked her."

"What would you do if you went on the best date of your life?" Clint asked, smirking at Jackson as his team drove the lane and scored a layup.

"Tell my friends," Reed said.

"Just do the math," he said. "You've been on thousands of dates, and if each girl just told twenty friends? You're talking thousands that know about you. You're an urban legend by now."

"I'm surprised it took this long for it to get public," Jackson said. "You've done a pretty good job of flying under the radar."

"I'm talking about dating with Rapunzel and a Silver Bullet," Reed said. "I may need to rethink my life choices."

Jackson and Clint grinned at each other, and then Jackson said, "Why does it matter if girls know?"

Reed thought back to the girls he'd dated prior to Kate, several of whom had known about his dating habits. It had proved to be a double-edged sword, with most dates already accepting the no-intimacy rule, while a few girls had been dead set on breaking him of his habit.

"Should I back off?" Reed asked, examining the paper again.

"Why?" Jackson said, sparing him a look. "What would that change?"

"I could just be a student," Reed said.

"Could you do it?" Jackson asked. "I mean, could you stop dating entirely and just do schoolwork and work?"

"I graduate in December," he said. "Then I'm not going to be in Boulder anymore."

"Could you do it to Kate?"

Reed fell silent, but one of the girls had committed a hard foul and Clint and Jackson leapt to their feet, both shouting at the ref. He was another student and had apparently refereed enough games to know both Clint and Jackson. He made the call and then stabbed a finger to Jackson and Clint.

"Sit down, girls."

"I hate that ref," Jackson said.

"Me too," Clint said.

Reed watched the game, his mind on Kate. On their last date he'd come insanely close to holding her hand, and he'd begun to wonder if his willpower could endure much longer. He hadn't told Jackson about the moment because his roommate would laugh in his face. Sex was a common topic in college, so for a guy to be afraid to hold hands seemed ridiculous.

But for him it was an enormous boundary, one he'd maintained for so long that the prospect of crossing it was surprisingly terrifying. He frowned at his own fears and recalled that, in the moment, he had not been afraid. Instead he'd felt excited, nervous, and hopeful.

"What have I gotten myself into?" he asked aloud.

Clint grinned and looked at him. "You never plan to fall for a girl," he said. "It happens to all of us. The question is whether or not you crash and burn."

"Which also happens to all of us," Jackson said.

Reed pointed to the picture. "We're clearly going to play Truth or Dare."

Clint smirked. "Your version of Truth or Dare is so bland it's probably a baked potato."

"Without butter or cheese," Jackson agreed.

"Whose side are you on?" Reed asked.

"Hers," they said in unison, and Jackson added, "It's her week, remember?"

"Did you tell her I was at the library?"

He grinned. "Guilty."

"I'm going to stop telling you where I'm going," Reed said.

"Don't do that," Clint said. "I like reading about you in the paper."

Reed leaned back in his seat and watched the game. The Silver Bullets were up by three, but the game was close, and likely to stay close throughout. Both Clint and Jackson were on the edge of their seats, as if being a few inches closer to the game could ensure victory.

Reed examined his friends, wondering if they had something he did not. They were both in stable relationships, and were confident enough to dress ridiculously to support their girlfriends. As much as Reed had dated, he had very little experience with what to do with a girl he desperately wanted to be with.

He fleetingly wondered what Aura would want him to do. Would she want him to give up all pretense and stay with Kate? Or continue to fulfill his promise? He sighed, realizing that as much as he needed the answer, he still felt torn.

As the game passed halftime, his thoughts shifted to his upcoming date. His anticipation at more time with Kate was tempered by his worry about the game. He wasn't concerned about the dares, he felt he knew her well enough to know they would not be outrageous. It was the truths he feared.

Chapter 34

The following Thursday Reed got ready for Kate's arrival, vacillating between worry and excitement. When the doorbell rang, Reed donned his jacket and joined Kate on the porch. He smiled, relieved to feel all his concerns melting away. She smiled back at him and led the way to her car, where she opened the door for him.

"I hope you're ready," she said.

"Your invite wasn't subtle," he said.

She grinned. "I was actually in the library on the balcony above you."

"Really?" he asked.

"I wouldn't have missed it," she said, backing out of the driveway.

"Who did Ember threaten to get the band to come?"

Kate laughed and inclined her head. "A good guess, but this time it didn't require any threats. Marta's cousin is the drum major, and they all have to listen to him. When we were discussing ideas for this week he called to ask Marta for a favor, and it all dominoed from there."

"Watching the band try to be quiet was epic," he said. "Well played."

"Thank you," she said. "Ready for dinner?"

"Should I be afraid?"

"Not if you like sushi."

She cast him a look, evidently to gauge his reaction. "Never had it," he admitted.

"Really?" she asked, clearly surprised.

"I've had dates who loved it," he said, "but I've managed to avoid it."

"Do you not like fish?" she asked, a trace of nervousness seeping into her voice.

"I like fish," he said, "but raw seafood has never sounded appealing. But I'm game to try it with you."

"Good," she said, her confidence returning. "I'm glad I get to be your guide."

"Be gentle," he said.

She laughed and turned onto the highway that took them downtown. For a moment there was silence in the car, the strangeness of the quiet causing Reed to sneak a look. The usual lightness to Kate's expression was absent. He wanted to ask what was wrong, but she launched into an explanation of the types of food they would encounter at dinner.

"We're going to try a variety of sushi," she said. "And before you ask, I've only had it a few times, so I'm going to be eating things I've never tried before."

"You've shown quite the sense of adventure," he said. "But I didn't realize it extended to food."

She smiled. "This is our ten-week anniversary of not-dating," she said. "I figured a truth or dare game would help us dive a little deeper."

"Is everything okay?" he asked on impulse.

"Fine," she said, not quite convincingly.

Resolving to be patient, he asked, "Tell me more about what we're going to be eating. Is it really raw?"

She pointed to a folder against his seat. "I took the liberty of printing off a list for us to look at. It's quite detailed, so it will help us decide what we want to try."

He scanned the list, uncertain if any of it sounded appetizing. Some contained eel, crab, shrimp, or tuna. Other names were unfamiliar, such as sashimi, nigiri, and maki. When he got to the bottom he looked up to find Kate smiling at him.

"Ready for the first dare?"

"Can I say no?"

She laughed. "No."

"Then let's do this," he said.

They exited the car and stepped to the shop. Upon entry, a waitress took them to a corner table. Apparently their arrival was anticipated, because the girl already knew they didn't have much experience with sushi. After describing several dishes, she left to get their drinks.

He leaned in, his eyes narrowing. "You already knew I've never had sushi."

Her smile was wicked. "You talked to my mother. I talked to yours."

"I'm guessing Jackson gave you her number?"

"Of course," Kate said.

Reed laughed in chagrin. "I honestly don't know which I like more, having all the power when it's my turn to ask, or the surprise when it's your turn. You saw that your invite made the school paper?"

She flushed. "I didn't expect that."

"It's one of the cleverest invitations I've seen," he said. "You deserve praise for it."

"I'll have to be more subtle in the future," she said, and then her brow knit together. "Wait, you said the cleverest you've *seen*. Do others do this creative dating?"

"You've caught me." He smiled and lowered his tone. "I belong to a secret society called the Creative Daters. It's kind of like the mob, except we have less secret beatings and death."

193

"The mob?" she asked, raising an eyebrow.

"Of course," he said. "We should have inducted you earlier, but I've been busy."

"Is there a ceremony or something?"

"In our secret sanctum," he replied.

"What else do you do there?" she asked.

"We plan our attacks," he said it like it was obvious. "We're sworn enemies of the Haters."

"I think Taylor Swift sang about them," she said, her lips twitching with amusement.

"She's one of us," he said. "Most of her songs are secret messages for the Daters."

She couldn't hold it in anymore and began to laugh. "Seriously, are there others that do this?"

"I've told you about my master's thesis," he said. "I've had a few friends start creative dating."

"And?"

He smiled. "All three are now married. One has a kid. He was actually the one to suggest I study it for my thesis."

Their food came to the table, interrupting their conversation. Kate had ordered a platter with a variety of sushi and he examined them at a distance, trying to identify them by color. Then he remembered the paper Kate had prepared and laid it next to the platter.

For the next several minutes they identified what was on the platter, as well as what was apparently called wasabi, about which Kate provided a word of warning. Taking a pink Maki roll and dipping it into the wasabi, he took an experimental bite.

The spice hit him first, followed by the strange taste and texture of the fish. He grimaced. She laughed and chose her own, which she identified as a California Roll. Avoiding the wasabi, she took a bite.

194

"It wasn't bad," Reed said, swallowing.

"Liar," she said, and then pointed to her selection. "This is good."

He took the second California Roll and added just a touch of wasabi. This time it was better and he nodded in approval. Once he got past the texture the taste wasn't too bad. She smiled at his expression and chose one identified as Nigiri.

"At the same time?" she asked.

"Is that a dare?"

Her smile became challenging. "Of course."

He grinned and picked up the second one. Foregoing the wasabi, he ate it by itself. They grimaced in unison, and both tried not to laugh. After drinking some water to banish the taste, they proceeded to try the other types on the plate, progressing to those that looked more exotic.

Not in a rush, they laughed at each other's responses and sampled their way through the platter. Partway through the meal he dared her to use chopsticks, resulting in several bites of sushi ending up on the table.

"Ready for the second course?" she asked as they finished the last on the platter.

"There's more?"

Her eyes twinkled. "That was the normal types. Now it gets interesting."

"What does that mean?" he asked cautiously.

His question was answered when the waitress returned with a second, smaller platter. He consulted the list and found them. His expression turned incredulous as he read the names and descriptions.

"Octopus? Eel?"

She grinned. "I've never tried them either."

"But you're making me try them?"

"That's the game," she said. "Are you giving up?"

"I'd rather choose a truth," he said, poking the octopus with his chopstick.

"That comes later," she said.

"Oh?"

"Didn't I say?" she asked. "The dares come first. Then the truth."

Her tone was amused, but there was a flicker of seriousness in her gaze, as if she had an ulterior motive. He wondered if it had anything to do with what was bothering her and decided that perhaps the game would allow him to learn.

Shaking his head, he picked up the eel. "Unakyu is cooked, at least," he said.

She took the second one off the platter and balanced it on her chopsticks. "Ready?"

"No."

She laughed. "Three, two, one . . ."

He put it into his mouth but she dropped hers, causing him to stab an accusing finger at her. She managed to catch it and eat, and then noticed his expression. An instant later hers became the same.

"What have you done to me?" he spoke through a mouthful of food.

She shrugged sheepishly and reached for her water. She swallowed and then said, "It was worth it to see your face."

He grinned, but behind his smile he watched her eyes, wondering about the truth to come.

Chapter 35

"Is a hamburger out of the question?" he asked.

They'd just finished the sushi, or more accurately, he'd taken a nibble of each of the more exotic ones on the plate. Most of it remained but he couldn't bring himself to eat any more. He felt a little queasy, although some of the sushi had been delicious.

"You look a little green," she said.

"That's the wasabi."

She laughed. "Some of it was good."

"Well put," he said.

"The octopus?"

Reed shook his head. "On the plus side, the taste has cemented the moment into memory, so I will always remember you."

"Along with the taste of fish," she said.

"You were already unforgettable," he said. "You didn't need octopus to get you there."

"A girl has to hedge her bets," she said.

"Not one like you."

He said it with amusement, but her return smile was brief and she focused her attention on the check. She seemed to linger on the check as if wanting to regain her composure. As they walked outside he stole a look. He'd all but forgotten her previous quiet but now realized that whatever was weighing on her mind, the sushi dinner had failed to alleviate the burden.

"Ready for the activity?" she asked.

"Anything but fish," he said fervently.

"How about eggs?" she asked with a laugh.

"Dates are supposed to be fun," he said.

"It will be," she said. "You won't be eating these eggs."

He raised an eyebrow but she merely laughed and opened his door. Once they were in the car, she left downtown and headed back to campus. He tried to imagine what exactly they'd be doing with eggs but could not picture anything good. Still, her smile of anticipation was reason enough to think it would be.

She drove them to her house and parked in the driveway. As they walked to the front he recalled Hogwarts and wondered if he would ever meet a girl so inventive. Seeming to think the same thoughts, she sighed in regret.

"We left the starry night up for a week," she said. "And two of my roommates planned their own dates around it."

"Ember?" he asked.

"And Brittney," she said. "Before your date, they used the Harry Potter decorations as well. Marta claimed that bringing a man into the wizarding world of our house would sully the décor."

"She didn't find a date."

Kate laughed, the tone indicating he'd guessed right. "She didn't get a date," she confirmed. "But it wasn't all her fault. She had to work most nights because one of her cousins was sick."

"I've been meaning to ask," he said as they stepped into the house. "What do your roommates think of all this . . .?"

He came to a stop as he realized that much of the room was covered in sheets of plastic. The material covered the couches and even the walls. Only two chairs faced each other at the center of the room.

"Do our eggs come with a side of murder?" he asked.

She grinned and gestured for him to take a seat. A small table sat between them. From the fridge, she retrieved four cartons of eggs, which she placed on the table between them. After opening them both, she brought out haircutting aprons and tied one around his neck. Then she donned her own and sat down, making the plastic crinkle.

"No knives or guns?"

"Half the eggs are raw," she said, "so I anticipate quite a mess."

She placed a set of cards between the two cartons of eggs. "You draw a card and have a choice," she said. "You can either answer, or take an egg."

"To the face?"

"No," she said with a laugh. "You'll crush it on top of your head."

"Where'd you get the cards?"

"Don't worry," she said. "My roommates removed the cards they deemed too risqué."

"Why?" he asked. "It would have been fun."

She snorted in disagreement. "All of your answers would have been no, so it would have given you an advantage."

"I could have learned interesting things about you," he pointed out.

She flushed. "Not things I want you to know."

He grinned, and then caught what she'd said earlier. "Wait, you haven't seen the cards?"

"I didn't want to give myself a chance to prepare answers," she said, "and if I'd read the questions, I would already know what to expect. A game of truth can't be real if you already know the answers."

"I'm impressed," he said, and meant it. "I would have looked."

"I would have as well," she said. "But Ember insisted. She keeps trying to take over my dates, you know." Then Kate gestured to the cards in invitation.

"Shouldn't the lady go first?" he asked.

"I asked you," she said, her lips twitching. "So that means you go first."

He couldn't argue with that, so he picked up a card and read aloud. "What's your greatest fear?"

She looked at him expectantly as he considered the question. Although there were several things he was afraid of, a few were not worth admitting. But the demands of the game compelled him to answer.

"I guess I would say losing my sister," he said.

"I expected spiders or something," she said.

"My sister is amazing, but she wants to be a traveling doctor," Reed said. "And I'm afraid that if she goes to Africa or South America I'll never see her again."

"She's not afraid?"

Reed shook his head. "She's fearless, and has even talked about going to Afghanistan or Turkey to help with the refugees."

"She sounds brave," Kate said.

"She's brave bottled into a tiny girl," Reed said. "But I believe I answered your question. Your turn."

She picked it up and read it to herself. She did not share the card but her expression betrayed her hesitation. Her eyes flicked to Reed and then the eggs, revealing her desire to avoid telling the truth.

"I'll take an egg," she said.

"How bad can it be?" he asked. "And I read my question out loud."

"You don't have to," she said.

"Changing the rule in the middle?" he protested. "I call foul."

She relented with a sigh and read the card. "What's a rumor you intentionally participated in?"

"Is it bad?"

"Very," Kate admitted. "Let's just say I was different in middle school."

She picked up an egg and steeled herself, and then crushed it on her head. The shell shattered and hard-boiled egg crumbled into her hair. She sighed in relief and brushed it off as Reed laughed.

"I think I like the egg more than the truth."

"Your turn," she said.

He drew the next card and read, "What is the thing you are most ashamed of?"

"This ought to be good."

"I'm going to take an egg," he said with a laugh.

"How bad could it be?"

"Bad enough I'm going to take my chances with an egg," he said with a smile.

He chose one from the other carton and tried to gauge its weight. When it was clear the effort was futile, he held it above his head and prepared himself. Then he crushed it on his head, sending raw egg exploding into his hair.

His cry of dismay was only matched by Kate's delight. Groaning, he sought to clean the disgusting muck from his hair. A bit of yolk ran down his cheek and he scraped it off and flicked it at her.

"This is disgustingly fun," he said.

"Not for the one watching it," she said, and then smirked. "For me it was just fun."

She reached down and drew the next card, which proved to be a question about regret. As they worked their way through the cards they both answered some, and both ended up decorated with egg.

Initially, Kate did far better. Then she took three eggs in a row, the last of which burst so wide that it splattered Reed. He laughed and tried to ward off the spray but she spun her head, sending more his way.

"You've got more hair to do that," he protested, trying to block the sprays of egg and shell.

"A smart girl uses her hair as a weapon," she said, her attempts at cleaning her hair succeeding only in spreading the mess.

"She does at that," he said. "But I don't think hair is usually colored with egg."

"True," she allowed.

He picked up a card. "Were you ever in love?"

"What a great question," she said.

"How would you answer it?" he asked.

"Not my card," she said, shaking her head. "Besides, Jason was the only one I've been in love with, so it would have been an easy answer."

He hesitated, sensing a weight to the question that went beyond the game. To take an egg would be an obvious attempt to hide the truth, and doing so would make her distrust him. Realizing he had no choice, he nodded.

"Once," he said. "But I already told you about Aura."

Chapter 36

"You've mentioned her before," Kate said. "But I didn't realize you loved her."

"We went on a grand total of one date," he said. "And it didn't last long. She never knew how strongly I felt."

"You did go on a date, though."

"If you can call it that," he replied. "I convinced her to have dinner with me but she was still dating Tim. As I said before, the start of their relationship proved the end of ours."

"Why didn't you ever tell her what you felt?"

"I started to," he said. "But when I tried, she told me to stop. She said she didn't want to ruin our friendship."

"Attraction has a way of ruining friendships," she said in agreement.

"I really thought we were fated for each other," he said, and then smiled wryly. "But I was young, so how could I really know?"

"How long did you feel that way?"

"Three years," he said.

"Not a crush," Kate said. "Those never last long."

He shrugged and glanced down at the forgotten eggs. It felt odd to talk about Aura with Kate, and he wanted to tell her everything—and end the conversation as quickly as possible. As if sensing the concern behind the loss, she gestured to the cards.

"We could move on if you want," she said.

"I think I'm about done with eggs," he replied.

"Me too," she said, and then her smile turned mischievous. "But we might as well use them."

She picked up an egg and threw it at him. It missed and shattered on the plastic covered wall, the yolk spraying the room. He flinched as it flew past his ear and then picked up a carton of eggs. He threw one at her and it broke on her stomach, but it was hard boiled.

"I can't believe you threw an egg at me!"

"I can't believe I missed!" she said.

She caught the other carton and ducked behind a chair. He did the same as they both unloaded the eggs in a flurry. With just a few eggs each, they were done in seconds, with both taking hits from raw and cooked. When it finished they were both laughing. As he made to stand there was a click at the door, and it swung open to reveal Marta.

"Sorry," she said. "I just got off work and . . ."

Marta froze as she caught sight of them. Her eyes took in the room and settled on them, both frozen behind the chairs. With egg streaming down their bodies and splattered across the plastic, they looked like they'd been at war with chickens. And lost.

Then Marta's weariness turned to delight and she whipped out her phone. "Smile!" she said brightly.

"Marta, no!" Kate said in horror.

"Too late!" she said, stuffing her phone back into her pocket.

"I can explain," Kate said.

"No need," Marta said. "You've caught me in more compromising—but less foody—situations. Enjoy your date!"

"I think we should hug her to welcome her home," Reed said. "Doesn't she look tired?"

Kate spread her arms wide, dripping egg white onto the plastic covering the couch. "Welcome home, Marta!"

Marta beat a hasty retreat, and when the door shut they dissolved into laughter until they surveyed the room, where egg covered nearly every stretch of plastic. Then she sighed and wiped her face.

"Ready to get cleaned up?"

"I was ready after the first egg," he said.

She led him outside to the hose and they took turns hosing each other off. Then they went back inside and carefully rolled up the plastic and loaded it into the trash outside. Neither felt clean, so they went back outside and used shampoo and cleaned their hair further. Finally devoid of egg, they stood and surveyed the plastic free room.

"Better," she said.

"I think we should have left it for the blondes," he said.

She smiled and shook her head. "Ready for the treat?"

"I'm afraid to ask what it is, after raw fish and raw eggs. I'm starting to see a pattern."

"This one I think you'll like," she said. "Or at least I hope you will."

They returned to her car and she drove them down the street. He expected them to drive further but she stopped at the Wendy's on the corner. When they stepped inside she ordered two Frostys and large fries.

"Are we dipping the fries into ice cream?" he asked, but the hope in his voice gave him away.

"I used to love doing this as a kid," she said.

"Me too," he replied.

They took a seat in the corner, but they had the place mostly to themselves. They'd spent a great deal of time at the restaurant and it had taken time to clean up the egg fight. The late hour left them alone, except for an older man sipping coffee and reading.

They both dipped their fries into their Frostys and grinned in unison. After the crazy food of the night the taste of hot and salty with cold and sweet was heavenly, and for several moments they couldn't speak through the food in their mouths.

"You never answered my question," he finally said. "What do your roommates think of our challenge?"

"Honestly?" she asked. "They think I'm falling for you."

"Are you?" he asked with a smile.

"We're only on our sixth date," she said, dodging the question.

Her phone pinged and she pulled it out. The angle didn't allow him to see the screen, but whatever it was made her smile falter. It was the third time he'd seen that look during the evening, but she put her phone away and turned her attention to her fries.

"I like the chocolate Frosty," she said. "But the vanilla's good too."

"Do you want to talk about it?" he asked.

"Talk about what?"

"Whatever is causing your smile to be forced."

"It's not—I'm just . . ." She blew out her breath. "Is it that obvious?"

"No," he assured her. "But I like to think I know how to read you by now."

She played with a fry, her eyes hesitant. The man in the corner turned the page of his book and sipped his coffee, the workers behind the counter laughed at something the cook had said. Then Kate met his gaze.

"Jason is coming back to Boulder."

It felt like a fishhook had yanked on his stomach. The surge of emotion surprised him, but she was watching to gauge his reaction, so he forced a shrug, giving himself time to figure out an appropriate response.

"What does he want?" he asked.

"I'm not sure," she said. "He's flying back in two weeks and wants to get together."

"You don't have to ask my permission," he said.

"I know," she said, absently stirring her ice cream with a spoon. "I just don't know what to do."

"What do the blondes say?"

She smiled faintly at his use of the nickname she'd given them. "They think I should say no."

"And what do you think?"

"I'm torn," she admitted. "When he asked me to meet I was relieved. I didn't realize I'd missed him so much."

"Go with him," he said, even though it hurt to say the words.

She regarded him, her eyebrows pulling together. "Why would you say that?"

"If you don't, you'll regret it," he said. "And if you do go, you'll figure out what you feel for him."

"Sound advice."

"I do try," he said.

They smiled at each other, but their conversation had cooled. He pretended to hunt for fries in the empty carton and exulted when he found two. He dropped them into his cup and picked them back up with his spoon.

"Go with him," he repeated. "We can take a break from our game."

"So, we're not going to talk for a month?"

"Not going to *date* for a month," he corrected.

Her expression revealed disappointment, but it disappeared as she drained the last of her frosty. Then she rose to her feet and threw it away. Following her lead, he did the same and then walked with her to her car. Unable to resist, he surreptitiously withdrew his phone and texted five words. Kate's phone pinged as she turned on the car and she pulled it out to read the text.

Doesn't mean we can't talk.

She smiled and looked to him. "It's about time."

He laughed. "Don't reply while you're driving."

She smiled in agreement and turned onto the road. He couldn't be sure, but it seemed she was lighter on the drive back to his house. When they arrived, she walked him to the door and they hugged, the embrace lasting several moments longer than necessary. When they parted she smiled faintly.

"It may come two weeks later," she said, "but stay tuned for my invite."

"Nope," he said. "I already have mine planned, so you're going to have to wait your turn."

She grinned. "Then I await your invitation."

As she drove away he wondered if she'd meant more.

Chapter 37

"How was the sushi?" Jackson asked as Reed entered the house.

"Don't try the octopus," he said.

"You tried *octopus*?" Shelby asked.

They were sitting on the couch watching a movie, popcorn and the remains of root beer floats on the coffee table. Reed sank onto the couch with a sigh and watched the screen without seeing it.

"How was Truth or Dare?" Jackson asked.

"Fun," he replied.

Shelby's expression was doubtful. "Without the fun cards I'm sure it was actually rather tame."

"You know that Ember took the cards out?" he asked.

"I told you," Jackson said. "We know everything. Besides, she gave them to us and we had fun."

"You should try it with eggs," Reed said.

"Hard pass," Jackson said, but Shelby smiled.

"Next time."

Jackson threw her a look and she shrugged. "It would have made it interesting," he said. "You kept trying to dodge questions."

"You're the one that discarded some when my back was turned," Shelby countered.

He grinned. "I thought I got away with that."

"Nope," Shelby said, and turned back to Reed. "How many eggs did you take?"

"Enough," he said in chagrin. "We ended up fighting over the rest. Egg was everywhere by the time it was over."

"We know," Shelby said. "Marta posted it and the image says it all."

"Of course she did," Reed said.

He pulled out his phone and checked to see if he'd been tagged in the photo. They were both covered in egg and Kate had her hand raised as if it would stop the photo from being taken. Reed was in the back, laughing at the absurdity of the moment. The comments were already calling it the Chicken War.

"Want to join us?" Jackson asked, gesturing to the movie. "We'd love to hear about it."

"You two are like parents waiting up for their kid."

"We've taught him well," Jackson said with a patriarchal voice. "He knows to keep the lights and pants on."

"Have you really never had sex?" Shelby asked, here eyebrows rising.

"Shelby," Jackson said in exasperation. "You can't just ask a guy that."

"Sorry," Shelby said. "But really?"

"Nope," Reed said.

"That puts a whole new spin on this," Shelby said, leaning forward. "Tell us everything."

"Tomorrow," Reed promised. "The octopus didn't like being eaten."

They exchanged a look but it was of curiosity, and he realized they noticed his melancholy. Before they could ask, he stood and went to his room. So they wouldn't think he was upset, he cast a casual comment over his shoulder.

"I think I still have egg in my hair," he said. "I'm going to take a shower and go to bed."

"Goodnight," they said in unison.

He stepped into his room and shut the door before sinking into a seat at his desk. As he did, his phone pinged and he pulled it out. He smiled softly when he noticed the message was from Kate.

I had a good time tonight, she said.

It was an adventure, he replied. **But next time I think we can skip the raw foods**.

Agreed.

He paused and looked at the screen, and then replied, **I won't invite you until after your date with Jason, so you can rest easy this week**.

Thank you for being honest.

I'll always be honest with you.

Promise?

He hesitated, and then said, **I promise**.

I'm still finding egg in my hair.

He grinned. **I hear it's good for the follicles**.

I hope so!

No reply came for several moments, and then she said, **Are you really okay with me going out with Jason?**

You need to go with him, and I think I can manage a few days without seeing you. He did not think it prudent to say he had other girls to go out with.

I don't know. You might fall apart without me.

I already am, he said, adding a smile so she would know it was not meant seriously.

Our picture is all over online. We look ridiculous.

Girls seem to think I'm cute with egg on my face.

It's a good look for you.

He grunted and shook his head. **Be careful with Jason. Seeing an ex can dredge up old feelings**.

Is that what it's like when you see Aura?

His smile faded and he stared at the screen. **I haven't seen her in years**, he said.

I'm sorry.

Me too.

But I'm not sorry we're texting.

I am, he said. **You're already a distraction.**

I've always wanted to be a distraction.

You are. He said. **A very pretty one.**

She responded with a smiley face emoji and a gif of a guy tripping because he was staring at a pretty girl. He smiled, pleased that they'd finally breached the texting barrier and then typed out a response.

Goodnight, Kate.

Goodnight Reed.

He wondered if there was something else she'd wanted to say but decided to end the conversation. Although he wanted to continue talking to her, he resisted the urge and put the phone down. Then he rubbed his face.

Now that he was alone he considered the hook that remained lodged in his abdomen. At first he'd thought it was just a protective urge, but as he considered his feelings it became clear he felt a different emotion.

Jealousy.

The realization caused him to lean back in his chair. He hadn't felt real jealousy since Aura, and he marveled at how much he suddenly hated Jason. The guy had lost his chance and shouldn't get another, but at the same time Reed knew it wasn't up to him.

As he lay in bed that night he found himself wondering if he'd revealed too much about Aura. He'd thought it would be hard to talk about—especially with Kate—but she'd listened without judgment and her smile had been one of understanding. Still, he'd withheld the darkest part of the story. Would she still think the same if she knew?

He frowned, wishing he knew what she was thinking. Was she more worried about her date with Jason? Or more worried about him? He hoped it was him—but at the same time recognized that if she decided to get back with Jason their game would come to a resounding end.

The sounds of Shelby's departure came shortly after and then Jackson went to bed. Like always, he crashed into the bed like a falling tree, and in minutes his muffled snores came through the wall. Still wrestling with his doubts, Reed rolled over and closed his eyes.

He didn't sleep.

Part 7: The Doctor Date

Chapter 38

Kate told herself she wasn't nervous. She went to class, helped a friend with her homework, and then did her own. She ate lunch with Ember at a café outside her work, and ignored Ember's snide comments about Jason.

"Can we please not talk about him?" Kate asked. "I'm fine."

"Then where's your laptop?" Ember asked.

"My what?" she asked. "It's right here . . ."

She reached to the back of her chair but her laptop bag was absent. She looked under her chair, her search becoming frantic when she realized it was not there. Grabbing her wallet, she fumbled for her credit card to pay the bill.

"I must have left it in class," she said.

"You did," Ember said.

Kate looked up to find Ember using her phone to show a picture of Brittney with Kate's laptop. The background of the selfie was clearly Kate's classroom, and the seat where she'd left the bag.

"I noticed you didn't have it when you got here," Ember said. "I texted Brittney and she picked it up after her class. You're lucky it was still there."

"Why didn't you tell me?" Kate demanded.

"We're fifteen minutes from campus," she said. "And Brittney was just getting out of class. She could get there faster than you could."

Kate wanted to be angry but she sank into her seat. "What am I supposed to do?"

"I'd punch Jason."

"You don't understand. When I got that text, everything came back, all the memories, everything I felt for him." Kate looked away. "I think I still love him."

"He's a great guy," Ember said. "It stands to reason why you would still feel that way."

Kate turned back in surprise. "I thought you hated him."

"I do," Ember said. "But not because he's a dog. He's actually one of the few guys I've met that's worth it."

"Then why do you hate him?"

Ember folded her arms. "Because he wasn't good enough for you."

"You just said he was a great guy."

"He is," Ember replied. "But that doesn't mean he's the right guy."

"Then why hate him?"

She sniffed. "Because he should have figured it out before proposing to you."

Kate laughed wryly. "Do you think I should go tonight?"

"Yes," Ember said. "It's the only way you'll ever realize he's not for you."

"And if I decide to get back with him?"

"Then I'll try to be nice at your wedding."

Kate sighed and looked down at her forgotten sandwich. The panini had cooled during their conversation, but she wasn't really hungry. She took a bite anyway, giving herself a moment to think.

Perhaps Ember was right. Jason had been her world for two years, a world that imploded the moment he'd proposed. She'd wondered a thousand times what would have happened if she'd said yes. Now would be her chance to find out. Her thoughts were interrupted when the waiter appeared.

"Can I get you the check?" the waiter asked.

He smiled, but there was a trace of irritation in his tone. Kate glanced to the front of the crowded restaurant and noticed a line of people waiting to be seated. She nodded and tried to swallow, but Ember spoke first.

"Grow a spine, would you?" Ember snapped. "If you want the table, just ask."

The guy flushed. "Just let me know when you're ready," he said, and scurried away.

Kate hid a smile. "That wasn't very nice."

"It was true," Ember said. "I was a waitress for six months—."

"—until you got fired."

"—and I never tried to rush a table. And I wasn't fired, I quit."

"You dumped a plate on a customer's head."

"He should have kept his hands to himself," she said.

"He was an attorney," Kate reminded her. "You're lucky you weren't sued."

Ember's smile was fond. "I'd forgotten about that. He threatened to have me thrown in jail."

"Why didn't he?" Kate asked.

"I took his fork and stabbed his steak so hard it broke the plate," she admitted. "Then I told him that when I got out I'd find him and teach him how to use his hands."

Kate laughed at the image of an attorney in a thousand-dollar suit cowering before Ember. The girl barely topped five feet but she could frighten the hide off a bear. Kate was grateful they were friends.

"One day your temper is going to come back to bite you," Kate said.

"Every girl has a spark of fire," Ember said. "Mine just happens to be hotter."

Kate smiled and took another bite, wondering if it was her own spark that had refused Jason's proposal. She liked to think she had a piece of Ember's courage. Even a part would be powerful.

They finished their meal and paid their bill to the now jittery waiter. Then they vacated the table for an impatient couple. When they exited the restaurant, they climbed into Ember's jeep and drove home. Mercifully, Ember talked about her latest boyfriend, a guy in the chess club who had no idea the wrath he was about to incur.

"He doesn't seem your usual type," Kate said.

"You should see him in a turtleneck," Ember said smugly. "He may be a nerd, but he works out like a wrestler."

"That sounds more like your type," Kate said with a smile.

"I'm taking him to a comic books shop," she said.

Kate frowned. "You're taking *him*?"

"I'd be getting social security by the time he asked," Ember said. "I followed your lead and asked him out. Reed gave me the idea about the comic book store."

"Just how much do you two talk?"

Ember shouted at a driver that was about to cut her off and then shrugged. "More when it's his turn to ask, but I've talked to him a few times about dating. His thesis is really intriguing."

"You're interested in psychology now?" Kate asked. "Since when did I step into bizarre world?"

"Most of the guys I date aren't exactly high quality," she said, her forehead knitting together. "I asked him why and he told me I might be looking in the wrong place."

"*He* sent you to the chess club?" she guessed.

"He dated a girl in the club and knew the members. He suggested I meet Tanner."

"Do you think I'm just a game to Reed?" Kate abruptly asked.

"If that's true, I'll kill him."

"No need for that," Kate said. "He's one of the best guys I've ever known."

"True," Ember said. "But that doesn't mean he hasn't made mistakes."

"Before we get to the beatings, can you answer the question?"

Ember was silent long enough that Kate glanced her way, but the girl's brow was furrowed in thought. She turned at a light, ignoring the honking car she'd just cut off and then accelerated down the street.

"No one does this much work for a friend," she said. "Even him."

"Then why do you sound uncertain?"

"I don't know," Ember said, her tone annoyed. "I just wonder if he's capable of dating just one girl. You must doubt it too, or you wouldn't have asked."

"I know he's attracted to me," she said, imagining Reed. "I see it in the way he looks at me, the way he smiles, the effort he puts into his dates."

"Then what are you afraid of?"

Kate watched the cars pass while she tried to get to the root of what bothered her. Every date with Reed cemented what she felt for him, and she suspected it did the same for him. But she couldn't shake a nagging doubt.

"Something drives him to date the way he does," she said. "And I still don't know what it is. I'm afraid he can't let it go . . . even for me."

"He hasn't told you?" Ember asked.

"I think it has to do with a girl named Aura," she said.

"Marta told me about her," Ember said. "What have you learned?"

"You should consider a career in law enforcement," Kate said. "You'd make a great cop."

"Too many rules," she said airily. "Besides, the truth is easier to get if you . . ." Her eyes narrowed. "Is that why you did the truth game?"

"Is that bad?" Kate asked.

"It's brilliant," Ember said.

"It wasn't the only reason," Kate said, feeling guilty. "But I did want to learn more about Aura."

"And?" Ember asked, pulling into the driveway.

"He was in love with her," Kate said.

Ember braked hard enough that Kate slammed into the seat belt. "He *what?*"

"She was his best friend for years but he fell for her," Kate said, rubbing her chest. "It's not like he's cheating on her."

"Oh," Ember said mildly, putting the car into park. "What happened between them?"

"Aura fell for a guy that pulled them apart."

"That's it?" she asked.

Kate hesitated. "I don't know. He talked about her with such . . . finality. I got the impression more happened than just losing a friend."

"Like what?"

"I'm not sure," she said.

She wondered if she could voice her suspicion. The way Reed talked about Aura, all in the past tense, even in his text, when he'd said

220

he hadn't seen her in a while, suggested something more than just the end of a friendship.

"I think Aura died," she said.

Chapter 39

Ember stared at her, her expression almost a scowl. "You think Reed was involved?"

"Not directly," Kate said. "But I think he feels responsible."

They sat in silence for several moments until Ember abruptly shrugged. "He'll tell you when he's ready."

"Why do you say that?"

"Because he's falling for you," Ember said. "Or else he never would have told you about Aura in the first place. A few more dates and he'll tell you everything."

"What if he doesn't?"

"Then let me go after him," Ember said.

Kate laughed and they exited the car. As they walked into the house Kate shook her head. "You don't need another restraining order. How many do you have now?"

"Don't knock my collection," she said, flipping her red hair. "Everyone has to have a hobby." She checked the time on her phone as she pulled out her keys. "You need to get ready. Jason said he'd pick you up at 4:00."

"That's three hours away."

"Do you know what you're going to wear?"

"No," she said.

"Then you'd better hurry," Ember said.

"I don't need three hours," Kate protested.

She was wrong.

"He'll be here any minute," Marta said.

"Stall him," Kate said, trying to finish her makeup.

"You sure you don't need more eye shadow?" Brittney said.

"You know I don't like makeup," Kate said.

She actually hated it, but endured the face altering creams, goops, and powders when necessary. And tonight it was definitely necessary. Still, she was pleased she'd kept it to her subdued style, just enough to enhance her natural features.

"Just a little more—" Brittney began.

"No time," Ember said.

"Thank you," Kate said, grateful for her support.

"Doesn't mean Brittney's wrong," Ember said, disappearing from the doorway.

Kate scowled, nearly poking herself in the eye with the eye liner. It had taken all of two hours to choose an outfit, one that satisfied all three of her roommates. The remaining time had been swallowed up by showering and doing her hair. The afternoon had been a blur of flying clothes and standing in front of the mirror.

"At least you look great," Marta said.

"That's because it's your top," she said.

"It should be yours," Marta said. "It looks better on you." She smiled and left, leaving Kate alone in the bathroom.

Kate put the eye liner down and stared at her reflection. Marta's top was a stunning green that matched Kate's eyes. The sleek material folded and tied across one breast down to her waist, where it wove into an artistically placed fold. The top accentuated her trim form while highlighting the curves of her chest and hips.

She wore her own jeans with Ember's belt, a wide black one that hugged her waist. Brittney had contributed the tie in her hair and the shoes, both of which were black. Kate had wanted to wear her sneakers, but she been overruled by her roommates.

"You have to look stunning yet unattainable," Ember had said.

"He has to regret ever letting you slip through his fingers," Marta agreed.

"He must forget every girl he's ever known," Brittney said.

Kate had begun protesting when Marta got home from work, but the blondes had all but forced her to strip and try on another outfit. Little remained in the closets, and piles of discarded clothing now rested on the beds.

"Flawless," Ember said when Kate stepped out in her current selection.

"Agreed," Brittney said.

Marta checked her phone. "He should be here any minute. You should have started getting ready earlier."

"Told you," Ember said.

The doorbell rang, startling Kate from her thoughts. She finished the eye liner and then stepped into the living room, shooing her roommates away so she could get the door herself. As she reached for the handle she steadied herself with a deep breath, and then swung the door open.

Dressed in stylish jeans, a long-sleeved shirt, and jacket, Jason stood on her porch for the first time in over a year. His blond hair was combed neatly, his blue eyes sharp and clear. With a chin like a block of concrete, he was every bit as gorgeous as she remembered.

"Kate," he said, and smiled.

"Hello, Jason," she said, and stepped into his open arms.

His arms wrapped around her and pulled her close. She breathed deep of his scent, a combination of leather from his car and his favorite cologne. The warmth of his chiseled chest enfolded her, eliciting a surge of memories that left her reeling.

She swallowed and reminded herself that they were not together. Then she extricated herself and looked up into his eyes. His smile was soft and inviting, but he spared a look into the house.

"Ember, Marta, Brittney," he said, his voice slightly less warm.

"Jason," Ember said, folding her arms.

"It's good to see you as well," he said. "But we'd better get going if we want to make our dinner reservation."

"We'll see you later," Brittney said.

"Don't be out too late," Marta added.

"I won't," Kate said, shutting the door on her roommates.

As they walked to the car his arm twitched like he wanted to hold her hand. He covered by pulling out his keys and pushing the button to unlock the car. He followed her around and opened her door.

"You're more beautiful than I remember," he said.

She paused behind the door and met his gaze. "You're not so bad yourself."

He laughed and waited for her to get in before shutting the door. He went around and got in, the mustang purring to life as he keyed the ignition. Then he eased the car onto the road and headed downtown.

"How is your conference going?" she asked.

"Great," he said. "A handful of the med students were picked to go, and I was one of the lucky ones."

"Does that mean you're doing well in school?" she asked.

"It's hard," Jason said. "But I like the studies. I'm thinking of going into pediatrics."

She raised an eyebrow. "A pediatric doctor?"

"What's so funny about that?" he asked.

"You had enough going for you as a doctor," she said. "Now you want to be a doctor for kids? You might as well scream perfect."

"Not perfect enough," he said.

She fell silent and looked away, uncertain as to the turn in conversation. Jason chuckled sourly. "Sorry. Seeing you has brought back a lot."

"For me too," Kate said quietly.

"Have you been dating?"

"Off and on," she said evasively. "You?"

"Not really," he said, his expression adding, *not since you.*

She cleared her throat and changed the subject. "What are your plans tonight?"

"Olive Garden," he said. "It was always one of your favorites."

She smiled, but found herself disappointed, her thoughts turning to the island dinner with Reed. The Italian food had been delicious, but probably not as good as her favorite restaurant. Still, she knew which had been more fun. Going back to Olive Garden somehow felt like a step backward.

"How's your school going?" he asked.

"The usual grind," Kate said, distracted. "I hate calculus, but love the applied classes."

"Everyone hates calculus," he said fervently.

He accelerated through a yellow light, and she said, "I see you still have your car."

"I don't have the heart to sell it," he said. "Even though my parents offered me a new one."

The Mustang had been a gift from his parents at his graduation. Both were doctors, one in radiology, the other a surgeon. Kate had imagined a life with Jason, visiting his parents, Jason's father stitching a cut on their child.

"How are Donna and Theo?" she asked.

"Getting a divorce," he said.

"Really?" she asked, shocked. "They were always so happy."

"I thought so too," he said, his voice tight. "I found out a couple of weeks ago, but they'd been separated for months."

Kate looked out the window at the lights of downtown Boulder, shaken. She wondered if marriage was even possible anymore, or were all relationships doomed to fail. Marta's parents were still together, as were Ember's. Brittney's mother had died from breast cancer and her dad remarried.

She glanced at Jason and saw the tension in his shoulders. Drawn to his pain, she reached out to touch his arm. "I'm sorry," she murmured. "I do know how you feel."

"When do you stop hoping for them to get back together?" he asked.

"I never stopped," she said.

He shook his head as he pulled into the Olive Garden. Then he parked and turned off the car, but remained in his seat, his shoulders hunched. After several moments he looked to Kate, his expression stricken.

"My dad cheated on my mom for years."

Kate reached over and wrapped her arms around his shoulders. Jason had always been strong, but now he seemed fragile, as if another blow could break him. She'd never seen him so crushed.

"I'm sorry," she murmured.

"I just don't understand," Jason said, his voice muffled through her hair.

Kate had no answers. She remembered a weekend with Donna and Theo. They'd been kind and fun, but looking back she recalled a lack of affection, of missed opportunities when they could have held hands, of glances without emotion. Abruptly Jason retreated and gestured to the restaurant, his smile forced.

"How about we skip the heavy talk and just enjoy dinner," he said.

"I'd like that," Kate said.

He smiled. "Me too."

It seemed he wanted to say more but then turned away and got out of the car. Kate watched him walk around, wondering if she'd made the right choice in coming, and wishing her heart would just decide.

Chapter 40

He came around the car and opened her door, and then walked her to the restaurant. They'd eaten at the restaurant many times in their time together, but she hadn't been back since they'd broken up.

Everything looked exactly the same. The smells were a delicious mix of olive oil, bread, and pasta. She breathed in and smiled, relishing the surge of memories, of them eating their favorite dishes, of kissing in his car, of what followed when they got back to his apartment …

She shook herself and looked at the chalkboard listing the specials. As Jason gave his name, the girl at the counter stole a look, her eyes traveling up and down Jason's body. Kate also noticed a passing waitress staring. Jason had always drawn attention, much to her amusement and consternation, but she was surprised to still feel a twinge of jealousy.

"Your table is ready," the girl said warmly, guiding them to a booth at the window.

"Thank you," Jason said politely, his smile causing her to turn a shade of pink.

They sat at the booth and Kate put the napkin on her leg. "You still have the same effect on girls."

He smiled. "It's the shirt."

"It's not the shirt."

His smile faded and it looked like he wanted to say something. Then his jaw tightened and he said, "Do you know what you want to order?"

"I haven't been here in a long time," she said. "Of course I want my favorite."

"Me too," he said. "Breadsticks."

She laughed lightly. "You always ate them all."

"I shared," he said indignantly, and then added. "Some."

"You hoarded the basket until you had to ask for more," she reminded him.

"Only once," he said.

"Twice," she replied.

He smiled but his reply went unvoiced when a server appeared. Apparently the new girl had been warned of Jason's presence and her gaze lingered on him as she took their order. Jason smoothly ordered for Kate as well as himself, something he'd done through much of their relationship. This time Kate found she didn't care for it, especially when he asked for wine for them both.

"Actually," she hedged. "I'd rather have water."

"Really?" Jason asked. "You used to love wine."

"I did," she said. "But I haven't really been drinking since . . ." She realized she was about to say *I started dating Reed* but caught herself in time. "Since February," she finished lamely.

Jason regarded her for a moment and then nodded. "Two waters, please."

The waitress nodded and took their menus. "Anything else I can get you?" She flashed a smile that suggested she wanted to give Jason much more than dinner.

"Some bread, please," he said.

"Coming right up," she said, and disappeared.

When she was gone he looked across the table. "What made you stop drinking?"

"I haven't," she said. "I just don't drink as often." She also wanted a clear head tonight.

She thought of Reed and why he didn't drink alcohol. He'd said his dad drank and she'd assumed that was the reason, but wondered if there was more to the story.

He gestured to her. "You seem different, more . . . forceful."

"You don't know the half of it," she said, thinking of the dates she'd orchestrated.

"I like it," Jason said. "You were always a little quiet, but now it's like you've lost what made you afraid."

"I wasn't afraid," she said.

Backpedaling from her expression, he shook his head. "You just seem more confident. It's a good look on you."

"Nice recovery," she said.

He feigned relief. "It's good to see you smile again. After . . . what happened, I thought I'd never see you again."

"I thought we weren't going to talk about heavy topics," she said.

"I just miss you," he said, leaning forward to take her hand.

She pulled away but smiled to take the sting from the action. "Your flirting is a little rusty."

He withdrew his hand but nodded. "I have all night to improve."

The bread came and for several minutes they talked of fun memories. She marveled at how much of their relationship now blended into a blur of movies and dinners, many of which had been at that very Olive Garden.

"Do you remember when we went to see *Batman v Superman*?"

"How can I forget?" she asked sourly.

He grinned. "You hated it, but I liked it."

"That's because you were never into comics," she said. "If you had, you would have hated the movie too."

"Soccer didn't give me much time," he said with a sigh. "Although I enjoy them now. Wonder Woman was amazing."

"Oh?"

"Can't a guy cheer for a beautiful woman with a sword?"

She smiled. "Perhaps."

He laughed and broke the warm breadstick in half, causing tendrils of steam to rise upward and dissipate. "How many times did you see Wonder Woman in the theatre?"

"Four," she admitted.

"Liar."

Kate smiled. "Seven."

He grinned, and she recalled their first date. He'd asked how many times she'd seen a recent movie and that had been their exact exchange. It was a callback to a perfect memory, and she wondered if it was intentional.

The salad arrived and Jason rebuffed the overly warm questions by the waitress. As Kate served a portion onto her plate, she struggled with the realization that Jason had never gotten over her, his eyes still harboring the same devoted focus he'd had when they were dating.

At the same time intoxicating and confusing, the sense that he still loved her sent her into an emotional tailspin, and for several moments she merely dodged his questions. As they finished their salad she looked up, abruptly deciding to voice her heart.

"Why did you want to see me tonight?"

"I told you," he said, obviously taken aback by her bold question. "I missed you."

"We both know it's more than that," she said.

He put his fork down and sat back in the booth, absently picking up another breadstick. He held her gaze without flinching, but she had to resist the urge to look away. As she waited, Kate considered Reed's words about courage, and wondered if he'd brought the attribute to the fore.

"I think you know," he finally said.

"I don't."

He put the bread down. "My feelings haven't changed," he said. "And I still don't understand why you ended it."

On her first date with Reed he'd described Kate's relationship as an old pair of sweat pants, comfortable, but who wants to spend their whole life in sweat pants? But how could she explain it to Jason?

"I did love you," she said. "But I don't want a future of Olive Gardens."

"You don't like Olive Garden now?" he asked.

"I love Olive Garden," Kate said. "But I just want . . ." She thought of her first date with Reed. "More."

"Do you want to go somewhere else?" he asked.

"No," she said, struggling with how to explain. "Why did you want to marry me?" she asked.

"Because I loved you," he said, his gaze adding, *and still do*.

She fumbled, struggling for a way to recover the conversation and regain control. "But what future did you imagine with me?" she asked.

"I don't know," he said. "Marriage, kids, a big house."

"And me?" she asked. "A doctor's wife?"

"Most girls would consider that a good thing," he said with a confident smile.

She smiled, grateful he had not been hurt by her words. He'd always had a gift with words, soothing hurt feelings as if it was as natural as breathing. It's what had made him a good captain on his soccer team, and part of the reason he would be an excellent doctor.

"This would be easier if you were a plumber."

He chuckled and brushed his hair back. Kate could have sworn she heard a nearby waitress suck her breath in but didn't look to find out. Kate knew she was floundering but could not think of what to say to escape. Jason merely munched on bread, a teasing smile on his face as he waited.

"The more you talk, the more you'll realize you made a mistake," he said.

She frowned, her confusion flickering to anger. "What mistake would that be?"

Realizing he'd spoken a bit carelessly, he swallowed and gestured in dismissal. "We both made a mistake," he said. "You don't need to go full Ember on me."

It was a joke they had shared in private before. They both knew Ember's temper and a simple reference was usually enough to elicit a smile. But after her conversation with Ember earlier, Kate did not smile. She folded her arms and leaned back. Jason was saved as their main course arrived.

Chapter 41

"Chicken Marsala for the lady, and Chicken and Shrimp Carbonara for the gentleman."

She put the plates on the table and offered parmesan, which Jason accepted while Kate declined. The girl stood with her hip almost touching Jason's shoulder as she churned the grinder, but Jason didn't spare her a look. When she left, Jason flashed a self-deprecating smile.

"I thought you liked parmesan."

"Not today."

Jason watched her for a moment and then chuckled. "You were a lily when I left and now you're a lion."

His smile was soft and apologetic, and her anger dissipated. "Sorry," she said.

He took a bite of his pasta. "What sparked this fire? And please don't say it was the end of our relationship."

"Actually, it had nothing to do with you," she said. "I met a—" She scrambled for the right word to describe Reed and settled on "—friend."

"What's his name?"

"How do you know it's a he?"

"Your hesitation."

She grunted and took a bite of her chicken. "His name is Reed. He took me on a couple of dates."

"I thought you said you weren't dating."

"I'm not," she said. "We haven't even kissed."

She knew she was attempting to mislead him, but told herself that she didn't have another way to describe her relationship with Reed. If she tried to explain the truth it would just result in both of them being confused.

"And he brought this courage out?"

"Unintentionally," she said. "His way of dating is . . . unique."

"Because he didn't kiss you?" He stopped eating and raised a quizzical eyebrow.

"He's just a good friend," she finished, hoping to end the conversation.

His eyes betrayed a trace of doubt, but he shrugged. "The change looks good on you," he said.

"You've said that before," she said.

"Really?" he asked, feigning confusion. "I was sure that was just a thought."

"Pretending like you're less intelligent then you are isn't going to work this time."

Caught, he grinned. "You were a good tutor."

"A tutor you didn't need."

"What did you expect me to do?" he asked, leaning in. "You were smart and beautiful but weren't into sports. I couldn't play the soccer player card because you didn't care. I had to come up with something else."

"Failing a quiz was a nice touch," she said.

"I still got an A in the class."

"You got something else," she said with a smile.

He returned it, the expression of a shared memory eliciting a flutter in her heart. He'd come to her pleading for help to improve his grade.

Their tutoring sessions had quickly evolved into more, and then she'd learned he had excellent grades. Her anger hadn't lasted long.

Jason had gone out of his way to spend time with her, and although time had made their relationship stagnate, it had not started that way. It surprised her to find a parallel between Jason and Reed. She wondered if dating Reed would produce the same result. Would he grow tired of dating the same girl?

He sipped his water. "Can I ask you a question?"

"What?" she asked.

"Have you missed me?"

"Yes."

She answered on impulse but spoke honestly. Fifteen months without him had done little to diminish the yearning, yet now she found that yearning had mingled with desire for another. She now wanted Reed. But who did she want more? And who would she want tomorrow?

Jason seemed satisfied with her answer and did not press the issue. Instead he took another bite and smiled as he chewed. Uncertain of what she was revealing, she focused on her own dinner.

"It's my turn to ask a question," she said.

His mouth was full, so he used a breadstick to gesture an invitation. She used the proximity to grab the second half of the breadstick, smiling as she popped it into her mouth. He snorted in disbelief and swallowed.

"That's the first time you've stolen my breadstick."

"I should have done it sooner," she said. "You always take the darker ones."

He laughed and shook his head. "What's your question?"

"Would you have dated me after we got married?"

His forehead knit together as he considered her question, and she realized it was not the question he'd anticipated. Content to wait, she took a bite of chicken, savoring the flavors she hadn't had since their breakup. She recalled eating the same meal the week before he'd proposed. That day she'd wondered why the food seemed to have lost its savor. Later she realized that she'd eaten the same meal so many times the flavor had faded.

"I don't think I understand your question," he finally said, shrugging helplessly.

"How would you date your wife?" she asked.

"You mean like go out to dinner?"

"Is that the extent of your plans?" she asked coyly.

"Some fun afterwards," he said with a smile.

"What about when you have kids and work and life are crazy? How would you date your wife then?"

"I think most people use babysitters," he said.

"Still dinner?" she pressed.

"I don't understand," he said. "Would you rather go to a club?"

She shook her head and looked away. "My parents used to go on a date night every week when I was little."

"I didn't know that."

"They gradually stopped, and a few years later they were divorced."

"Kate, sometimes a marriage just doesn't work out." His features tightened at the reminder of his parents.

"And we would have?" Kate asked, meeting his gaze.

"I'd like to think so," he replied. "But it would help if I knew what you wanted."

"What if I don't know what I want?"

"Then there's nothing I can do."

A car passed in the parking lot and she watched it turn onto the road. "I'm still trying to figure it out," she said.

"Kate," he said, drawing her gaze. He pulled out one of the darker breadsticks from the basket and handed it to her. "I can wait," he said.

Her heart fluttered but she did not look away. He smiled and nodded at her unflinching gaze. She also noticed a trace of desire before he looked away, and it stirred a familiar desire in her belly.

"Did you really not date anyone in the last year?" she asked.

"Is that so hard to believe?" he asked.

"Yes," she said. "I would expect another med student to snatch you up like a piece of chocolate."

"I do have a caramel filling," he said, nodding.

"So no nurses?" she asked.

"A few friends," he said. "Much like your Reed, I assume."

Not likely, she thought.

Noticing her doubt, he added, "It's not that they didn't try," he said. "I just found that my heart was elsewhere."

"On your studies?"

He smiled. "Maybe."

"What was her name?"

"Cindy," he said. "It lasted a few weeks. Then I ended it. Didn't feel fair to continue when she wanted more than I was willing to give."

Kate immediately disliked every Cindy she'd ever met. Then she recognized the surge of jealousy and suppressed it with difficulty. They were not together anymore, and he could date whoever she liked.

Just not Cindy.

"You know, you didn't have to transfer," she said. "You could have finished your bio program here."

Their conversation was warm and full of memories, as intoxicating as the wine she'd refused to drink. She needed to get sober before she went back to his hotel. At the same time she wondered if that would be so bad.

"Columbia has a great program," he said, avoiding the topic. "You know it was on my list."

"But you transferred because of our breakup," she said.

"Maybe," he said. "But now I'm trying to figure out what med school to go to. I've been accepted to the University of Colorado Denver School of Medicine."

She shook her head. "You've only been gone a year."

"I took an accelerated course load," he replied. "I finish at the end of the summer."

She frowned, finally putting the pieces together. He'd finished two years in just eighteen months, and was thinking of returning to Denver for med school—just thirty minutes from Boulder.

"That's what your conference is about," she accused.

"Guilty," he replied. "I was invited to Denver for a tour of their school."

"Just how much do they want you?"

"A lot," he said in a self-deprecating tone. "They seem to think my finishing early and my grades are indicative of a good doctor." He lowered his voice. "Don't tell them the real reason."

She took a sip of her water, trying to grasp the magnitude of everything he was saying—and not saying. Jason had finished early because of her, because she'd broken his heart. Now he had the chance to return to Colorado. He'd come to look at the school, but its program was not why he would accept. He wanted to return.

240

For her.

Chapter 42

As they left the restaurant she considered how easily they'd slipped back together. Over a year had passed and they still fit together— hand and glove. She even glanced down to make sure they weren't holding hands.

Despite the closeness she sensed a shift. It was difficult to discern at first, but the more time they spent together the more she realized they were not the same people they had been. He had always been the confident one, ever the captain even if he didn't have a team. She'd fallen into the position of his companion, his shadow.

She'd been okay with that—or thought she was. But the time apart and time with Reed had changed her, and she wasn't sure if she liked returning to Jason's shadow. She cast him a surreptitious look, wondering if what she felt was just a legacy from the past, or a lead for their future.

"What are you thinking about?" he asked.

"That you're a great guy."

"Really?"

"Yes."

He laughed and opened the passenger door. He shut it behind her and hurried to the driver's side. When he sat down he reached for the ignition, but she caught his hand, drawing his eyes to her. She withdrew her hand and shifted in her seat to face him.

"Why are you really here?" she asked.

He leaned back and raised an eyebrow. "I would think that would be obvious," he said. "I want you."

She shook her head. "I don't know if we still fit."

His voice softened. "I never stopped loving you, Kate."

She flushed. She'd known the answer but he'd said it aloud, unequivocally proclaimed in a fashion that could not be denied. He reached out and put a hand on her cheek. She shivered at the contact, but he was already pulling her in. She swallowed, her mind attempting to resist. His lips touched hers, tentative and restrained. He withdrew a moment and when she did not resist, leaned in again, the contact growing more ardent.

He pulled her against him, the space between them becoming an irritation as he brought her into a crushing embrace. His lips pressed against her and his hands roved across her back and sides, his hands filled with desperation.

But her mind would not stop, and thoughts spun like threads of smoke, dissipating as quickly as they came. Every time she gained her feet, the wave of desire dragged her under and she struggled to breathe.

Reed was the first thought, but she had no way to define what she felt for him, and the thought burned away. Then she randomly worried about how Ember would react if she started dating Jason again. Last, she felt a hardening in her stomach that had no name. In that moment Jason's hands moved upward, climbing up her body.

She gasped as the movement sent a thrill into her flesh. But this time it brought a screaming alarm with it, and she flinched. Her hand caught his, holding it fast before it could travel any higher.

He finally broke the kiss, but his lips remained close enough she could feel his breath. She struggled to find her center even as thoughts bombarded her. Both were breathing hard and when he spoke his voice was husky.

"My hotel is a few minutes away."

She saw her life unfold, a life of being with a doctor, of going to parties at the hospital, of the looks of jealousy from other women. She saw her weekends and herself getting pregnant, of years of her being at home . . .

But that is where the image came to an end. She didn't see if they would stay together or if she would become an engineer. She couldn't see if they would grow old together, visit their grandchildren, or dance together as a couple. Misunderstanding her silence as consent, he reached for the keys.

"Jason," she said.

She swallowed and leaned away from him, needing the space to gain clarity. Their eyes met, and he cringed at her expression. Then he shook his head and leaned against the door, his shoulders turning rigid.

"This used to be what you wanted."

"Now I want something more."

"I can be what you want," he said.

"I can't ask you to be what you aren't," she said. "You are wonderful the way you are, perfect in so many ways."

"But not perfect enough for you," he said, a trace of bitterness creeping into his voice.

"If we went back to your hotel it would be wonderful," she said. "We would get together, get married, and have a life."

"Is that so bad?"

"It would be beautiful," she said. "But I don't want to end up like my parents. Or like yours."

"We wouldn't get divorced," he said.

"This whole night we've talked about what we were," she said. "We didn't talk about what we weren't."

"Why did you say no?" he asked.

During dinner they'd been skirting the real issue, bantering about the past and not talking about why they'd ended. Now he'd asked the question he'd clearly harbored since their breakup, and his expression revealed a desperate need for an answer.

"Couples don't last," she said. "But I want to. I don't want to get divorced. I don't want to rip my family apart and be alone."

"I would never do that to you."

"Not intentionally," she said. "But you love me like I am now. What about when I'm a mom and pregnant and you are the handsome doctor all the nurses are in love with?"

"You think I'd cheat on you?"

"No," she said hastily, attempting to stop the hurt in his eyes. "But I think we'd be unhappy."

"You can't possibly know what we'd be like as a family," he protested. "For all you know, we'd grow old and die together."

"We fit now," she said. "But we've changed in a year. How can we know we'd still love each other in ten?"

"How can you not?" he asked. "I love this new strength of yours. I will always—"

"I don't think so," she said.

"What do you want, then?" he demanded. "I wanted to marry you."

"I don't just want a marriage," she said. "I want an eternity."

He regarded her with hard eyes. "What you want only exists in movies," he said.

"I hope not," she said fervently.

He grimaced and wiped a hand through his hair. "I would give anything to make you happy."

"Then find someone who makes you happy," she said.

"Kate," he said. "Can we just talk? Come back to my hotel and let's just keep talking."

"You know what we would do," she said quietly. "And if I did that I would lose myself to you."

"I love you," he said.

"I know," she said. "But in today's world, love isn't enough to keep two people together."

"Is this because of Reed?"

That caught her off guard, but she shook her head. "I said no to you because a part of me realized we weren't right for each other."

He released an explosive breath, his expression turning hard. "A lot of girls would be happy to be with me."

"Then choose one," she said. "It just won't be me."

"I can't believe you're doing this," he said, glaring at her. "I came all this way and all you can say is that you want something that doesn't exist? I thought I knew you better than that. I can't believe I thought you were smart."

Stung, she scowled, "I can't believe you're being stupid."

He snorted. "You're going to live your whole life wishing you'd stayed with me."

She watched him sit and seethe, the love she'd had for him finally beginning to wither. The doubt that had plagued her drained away and the desire to be with Jason went with it. She didn't know what lay in store between her and Reed, but it didn't matter. She wanted a future that Jason couldn't provide.

Ember had been right. Jason was a good guy, but was not the right guy. Kate didn't know who Reed would become or if they had a future together, but she wanted to find out. She needed to find out.

"I'm sorry, Jason," she said, and then reached for the door.

"You won't even let me take you home?" Surprise broke through his anger.

She looked back and met his gaze. "Goodbye Jason."

She exited the car and walked away. His door opened and he stood, and she expected him to call out to her, but his voice never came. She

246

turned the corner of the building as his car sped out of the parking lot, and she released a long breath.

She sank onto a bench at the front of the Olive Garden and pulled out her phone. Flipping to her favorites, she went to push Ember's number—but her thumb paused just above her name. On impulse she scrolled down to Reed and pressed. She swallowed as she put the phone to her ear.

"Kate?" he answered on the second ring. "Are you okay?"

She swallowed against the surge of tears. "Can you come pick me up, no questions asked?"

His answer was instant. "Always."

Chapter 43

Reed arrived fifteen minutes later, his old car chugging into the lot. Before he could get out, she opened the passenger side and slid in. Not daring to look at him, she buckled the seat belt and stared out the windshield as he pulled back on the road.

The seconds ticked by but he didn't speak, even though she could see the curiosity in his glances. Her courage failed her and she began to cry. She knew it was stupid, but all the emotion burgeoned to the surface and flooded onto her face.

Reed still didn't speak, and she was grateful for his silence. She cried quietly, relieved that it was over, wishing Jason hadn't been so hurt, wishing she hadn't been the one to hurt him. She wiped at the tears on her cheeks but more welled up, preventing her from seeing Reed park outside a different restaurant.

"Back in a moment," he said.

Startled, she looked to see him exiting the car, gone before she could speak. Not a minute later he returned and offered her a cup. She accepted it tentatively and looked to him, but he had a smile on his face.

"Hot chocolate," he said. "It makes everything better."

She couldn't help it, she laughed. She sipped the steaming liquid and felt the heat sink into her soul. Closing her eyes, she savored the heat all the way back home, grateful for the warmth that burned the tears from her eyes.

When they got to her house he walked her to her door. "I'll see you soon," he said.

"You really aren't going to ask any questions?" she asked.

"You asked me not to," he said.

"I just cried for fifteen minutes," she said.

"But you feel better now," he said.

"Yes."

"Then you can tell me when you're ready," he said. "I'm just glad you're okay."

"You can expect a new invite this week," she said.

"I thought we decided it was my turn."

She shook her head, marveling at the new foundation that had materialized beneath her. Jason may have caused a storm, but she'd also found her center. Wiping the lingering moisture from her face, she spoke with certainty.

"I'm sorry Jason took your turn," she said. "But I want the next turn—if you'll let me."

He regarded her for several seconds, his easy smile on his face, the expression warming her as much as the hot chocolate. She heard confidence in her voice and relished the newfound strength. Then he acquiesced with a nod.

His smile widened. "I look forward to it."

Kate watched him go and then entered her house where she was all but tackled by three furious women. She fended off their barrage of questions until Ember's voice finally cut through the din.

"You left with Jason and returned with Reed? What happened?"

"I ended it with Jason and Reed brought me home."

The girls hugged each other and Kate, pulling her into a burst of jubilation that almost spilled her hot chocolate. When she finally extricated herself Marta caught her hand, keeping her from escaping.

"How do you feel?"

Kate considered her answer and then smiled. "I feel free."

###

27 Dates: The Series

The Dating Challenge

The Dating Secret

The Dating Game

The Dating Handbook

The Dating Truth

Author Bio

Originally from Utah, Ben has grown up with a passion for learning. While still young, he practiced various sports, became an Eagle Scout, and taught himself to play the piano. As a teenager he began creative dating and continued the practice into college, where he took a break to do volunteer work in Brazil. After school, he launched his first series, The Chronicles of Lumineia, and has since published over 20 titles across multiple genres. He loves to snowboard, build treehouses, and play board games, especially with his family. His greatest support and inspiration comes from his wonderful wife and six beautiful children. Currently he resides in Missouri while working on his Masters in Professional Writing.

To contact the author, discover more about 27 Dates, or find out about the upcoming sequels, check out his website at 27Dates.com. You can also follow the author on twitter @27Dates or Facebook.